©2024 by T.Y. Ryan

All rights reserved. No part of this may be reproduced, distributed or transmitted in any form or by any means without prior written permission.

This is a work of fiction. Names, characters, places and incidents are a product of the author's imagination. Any resemblance to actual people, living or dead, or to businesses, events or locales is completely coincidental.

Contents

Chapter One

Chapter Two

Chapter Three

Chapter Four

Chapter Five

Chapter Six

Chapter Seven

Chapter Eight

Chapter Nine

Chapter Ten

Chapter One

Longwood, New Mexico, was a good ride from Boulder Pines, Colorado, but the time in the saddle hadn't done much for Nate Carson's mind. He remembered the day as clearly as anything in his life; it had been the one that had sent him off, after all.

It was five shots. *Five shots*. Five deaths. But three that made him an orphan and alone. Three that really mattered to him, though, given the tight-knit town, all five hurt. It was the three his mother, father, and brother took; those sunk a feeling in the back of his mind, in the front of his heart. Those were the ones he carried with him.

It had been seven years, but he still found himself up at night thinking, as if there was any point to it. What if he could've saved one? Or two? What if he had to pick?

Most nights, he thought he would've rather taken a bullet himself. At least then his mother or little brother would be alive. Raised by "Trusty Jim Carson," he knew the man would've insisted on being one to go down, even if his family wasn't at risk. That was just how Trusty Jim worked. If there was something tough to be done, he'd do it and then ask for more. It wasn't always the happiest home to grow up in, but it was one that instilled a hefty amount of integrity.

So Nate had laid awake at night, thinking.

He learned how to track down outlaws like the ones who stole his family. But he was still thinking.

And he finally found the information he needed. So he was riding back to Boulder Pines, thinking.

At first, it had just been a haggard, out-of-breath old man. Nate worked at the mercantile in Colorado back then. He was eighteen; his brother Matthew was three years younger. There wasn't much to be said about the town at that point. Most folks did their best to take care of it, and it took care of them. At that point, his biggest interests had been securing a good position at his job and, maybe, partially, catching the eye of Beth Ashwell, the pretty, sassy, smart little young lady who lived on the other side of town.

Truth be told, that had probably been his main goal for a good long time. She'd caught his eye the year before, when they'd both been turning eighteen. It was a funny coincidence, birthdays just three days apart, but it also meant he'd always known Beth. She was practically a sister after this long. But something about her one day, the way she'd done her hair, or the little smirk she gave to his jokes, something had stuck.

So, without quite admitting it to himself, and certainly not to anyone else, he'd taken the job at the general store. It wasn't entirely out of selfish reasons. He wanted to learn about business. He wanted to bring in some kind of income outside of what he did at the homestead for his folks. But mostly, he knew Beth Ashwell did her family's shopping, so if he wanted to be seeing more of her, that was pretty much the only place to go.

And it had worked, at least for a time. Unfortunately, barely a month after he'd taken the position, the man ran in.

"Your folks! Your brother!"

It was unnerving, to say the least. He knew the man by face, but couldn't quite place the name. Johnson, Jameson, something like that. And in the moment, it was probably the last thing he should've been worried about. The man was wheezing, leaning against the door frame of the mercantile, the bell above the door still ringing in the air.

"What about them?" Nate asked, discomfort and uncertainty fighting for a top place in his mind.

"The bank," Johnson or Jameson said. "You need to get over there!"

The man wasn't making anything easier for Nate, and the fact was, there were more than a few drunks in Boulder Pines at that point. It wasn't a large town, but every single one seemed to find its share, almost as if it was required.

Plus, it was the Ashwell's shopping day, and the fact that Beth usually did the shopping made him feel more than a little hesitant to jump at the ramblings of one of the town's old men.

"I can't leave the shop," Nate said, his voice hesitant. "What's wrong with the bank?"

He knew his parents weren't dropping dollars out of their pockets, but they were responsible. It was the only way he knew a person could be.

"Reese Gang," the man said, coughing, a hand to his stomach. "Made a run on the place."

He might've said more. It was one of the things Nate's mind tried to hone in on when he couldn't sleep, a useless detail that somehow applied and didn't apply to the thing he couldn't stop thinking about. What he knew was, he'd boosted himself up on the counter, swinging his legs over the wood and managing to knock the till cockeyed on the way. It was a pointless detail, but in the back of his mind, he knew if it spilled, he would cost the shop owner money, and if he cost the shop owner money, it would come out of his wages. And if money was coming out of his wages, even if he kept it to himself, Trusty Jim Carson would find out one way or another.

It had tilted, and he'd seen the man's glance, even as he tried to catch his breath, but when Nate shoved the door open, he very distinctly remembered the thud and clink as the register fell back.

It was the last memory of his old life.

Or maybe the first of his new one.

The Reese Gang didn't mean much to him. At least not until then. It was a name and a rumor, a reputation at best. Leon Reese was the kind of guy you heard about but almost barely believed in. He was a sketch in the back of your mind, a story more than a person. He'd worked his way from the panhandle in Oklahoma up toward Colorado, but still, somehow, that didn't mean he was real. There were plenty of other people to worry about, plenty of people in Boulder Pines itself. The same way they had their drunks, they had their outlaws, but typically, they were the same, and a drunk outlaw wasn't one you had to worry too much about.

Leon Reese, though…

It was only four buildings from the mercantile to the bank and Nate ran them faster than any horse could've taken him. His boot heels slammed on the wooden walkway as he raced toward the unknown.

"His momma was a rattlesnake and his daddy was a six-gun."

That's what Leon Reese wanted you to know; it's the story he wanted you to believe. It was the one the paper put out every week. But the paper never said anything about him coming to Colorado. Reese was a Texas outlaw, and whether it made sense or not, Nate felt like Texas could deal with their own problems; Colorado would deal with theirs.

But with one exhausted old man, he realized that what he thought didn't matter too terribly much, actually did matter.

The place was chaos when he arrived. A few deputies were outside, trying to keep people at bay, though one look at Nate got him waved inside. There were things to be said for keeping acquaintances. Deputy Rollins and he had been friends since they were in short pants, and this wasn't a moment either of them really wanted to deal with.

The sheriff was inside, talking to a clerk who was visibly shaking. A body lay on the floor, Mrs. Hancock, it looked like. Another, the new fella in town, not far from her. But to his right, back in a corner, he saw them.

At first the placement confused him, then his emotions dropped out and his logic kicked in. It actually made perfect sense. Matthew was the farthest back, then his mother, then his pa. Trusty Jim had pushed his wife and child back as far as he could, but they hadn't been close enough to the door to escape. And three bullets had done the rest.

Nate felt his legs go loose, but he refused to fall. This wasn't a situation that needed weakness; he could be sad later. Instead, he was angry. Rage filled.

He turned back to the sheriff, almost running across the room.

"Why are you still here?!" he yelled, breaking into whatever conversation the man was having. As far as Nate was concerned, nothing could be important enough to stand around and shoot the breeze about.

The man looked him up and down, seeming to almost purposefully take his time in answering. Nate knew him, in at least a general way, but at this point he wasn't terribly concerned about pleasantries.

"Well?"

The man pushed his hat back on his head, a gesture that showed both disinterest and a none-too-concealed attempt to put his star in Nate's sightline.

"Who let you in here?" the man asked.

What was it? Dawson? Dawkins? Nate's mind was scrambling for a name, scrambling for understanding, scrambling to stay clear. "I don't know if that's the question you ought to be asking," he said, keeping his voice as steady as he could.

"I've been asking questions. Quite a few good ones in fact, and…" his voice trailed off as realization dawned on his face, "You're the Carson boy."

Nate nodded, his jaw clenched. He knew it wasn't the sheriff's fault that this had happened. At least, not necessarily. But he wasn't sure how much chit-chat he was open to, given the pile of bodies in the corner.

"I'm so sorry, son," the sheriff reached out to put a hand on Nate's shoulder, but Nate shrugged it away.

"Sorry isn't doing us much good now, is it?"

"Listen, I can't imagine what you're feeling, but I think it's best you head on outta here. There's nothing you can do right now and being here isn't gonna make ya feel any better. You got any family in town?"

"Yeah," Nate spat. "A mother, a father, and a brother. Good thing you're here to keep 'em safe."

"Hey, now," the sheriff started, but Nate had already turned away. If he was going to get hassled about it, there was clearly time before the lawman finished up his jawing. The fella could track him down or let him be. It didn't matter then. Nothing did. One wheezing old man had been more help than the guy with the star on his chest.

The question now was, what next?

And what was next turned out to be a whirlwind of things.

Over the course of the next week, Nate's life changed almost entirely. The sheriff, while he was quite aware of who had committed the murders and the robbery, seemed to have very little interest in going after Leon Reese and his cohort. In fact, in a way that made Nate burn inside, the sheriff seemed to share the same opinion as Nate himself. The Reese Gang was a Texas problem, so Texas could take care of it.

"For all I know," the man had said, "they've headed back down south. We'll let that Texas justice knock 'em out. Them boys aren't any too friendly when it comes to the law down there."

So he'd been left in an odd position. Half the time he was at the mercantile, fuming, barely keeping his anger under control. The other half of the time, he was at home, in what felt like a ghost of a house. He still slept in his old room. He still sat in the same place at the table. But there was no one there. It was empty. Quiet. Everything looked as if his parents and brother should come back through the door at any moment, but the silence said otherwise.

He ate less. He slept less. He saw Beth Ashwell less. Not because he was avoiding her, but because the normal routine, the typical route to work, the one that took him a bit out of his way but closer to her, became less important. Maybe what he needed was a compassionate ear, but what he wanted was something else. He just couldn't figure out exactly what it was.

But, as things tend to go, *it* showed up on its own.

It had been almost three weeks since the Reese Gang had ridden into town and destroyed what Nate held dear. Off they'd gone, without so much as a slap on the wrist or even a flake of interest from the local law. The money was insured, after all. The deaths were unfortunate, but you just had to move on.

And maybe that was the west, but it wasn't the west he was willing to accept.

Nate sat in his usual chair at the dining table, very aware of the other three empty spaces. He knew he shouldn't be drinking coffee, not at almost midnight, but he also knew he had two choices: focus on the drink, or lay in bed and replay the same thoughts he'd had for almost a month now.

He could've been in the bank with them, but then what?

He could've paid more attention to what was happening outside, but he was at work.

The Reese Gang, for all he knew, looked like every other group of folks passing through. Maybe a little more suntanned, maybe a little rougher around the edges, but what was it that he was supposed to see?

The problem was, he'd missed something.

And when his head hit the pillow, that was the only thing he could think about.

So, coffee. At least this way he could critique himself for something he was in control of. If the milk was off, or if the flavor was mild, he understood how to fix it. It was the same with work. He could take money, make change, go through the motions. But the nights…the nights were long.

This one, however, played out a bit differently.

He was tapping his boot on the floor, a nervous habit he'd picked up but not really recognized until then. He was constantly in motion, tapping, picking at lint, brushing his pant legs, keeping his mind and his eyes occupied, so the sound didn't really ring with him at first.

But then it happened again.

He stopped his foot. The coffee was warm in its mug, but his hands began thrumming on the porcelain.

It wasn't a grunt. But it also wasn't the sound one of the horses would make. He sat in the stillness, listening.

It was a *creak*.

Before he quite knew what he was doing, Nate was up and headed to the door. He grabbed his gun belt off the peg on the wall, the one his father used to use, and strapped it on as he stomped across the porch.

It was only a few yards to the barn, just enough space to fit a wagon in. He'd always thought it was silly, but his mother had liked the convenience on the cold days and his father had acquiesced. Now he appreciated it in a new way.

The door to the barn was open, split above the padlock he'd been meticulously told to clasp every night. Things had changed in the last few weeks, but not everything. He touched it every night, giving the padlock a pull before going in and latching the front door behind him. They were pointless things now; he was the only one to take care of and he wasn't overly concerned about that. But they were the only things that still existed from a life he used to have. And now it had been changed.

He stood outside the barn door, listening for another tell-tale sound, but the night was silent. Maybe he'd imagined it. The air was cold and he wished he would've gotten his coat but…yes, there it was again. Not the sound of an animal, the sound of boots on hard-packed dirt. He put his hand to his revolver, drawing slowly from the holster. It would be ridiculous to think Reese had come back again, but at this point, he was ready to take his anger out on anyone stepping onto their land. Even if it wasn't technically 'theirs' anymore.

When he pulled the door open, the man was hunched over. He was obviously trying to finagle the latch on the stall door, but without light, he'd been working by feel more than thought. It should've been simple, Nate remembered thinking. Pull the gun, give the order, take the man in. But something had gone differently.

He never could quite say what it was. But there was something about the way the man stood, the movement of his body, his arms. Maybe it was just the frustration and anger that had been building. But Nate wasn't in a position to show patience.

The man stood and turned, and Nate fired.

He knew it wasn't a kill shot from the moment his finger touched the trigger. Trusty

Jim had raised him too well for that. But he knew where it was going and he knew what it would do.

The bullet took the man somewhere near the clavicle, with any luck, breaking it. The wound wasn't life-threatening, but it would put him on his back for a good bit of time. So, unless the fellow on the ground had more grit than most, he wasn't going anywhere.

Nate waved the smoke away from the barrel end and crossed the few steps through the barn entry.

"Got anything to say, or do you wanna leave this one up to the sheriff?"

"I was just passing through," the man grunted. It was a hopeless argument, one that didn't even really need recognizing.

"I'll help you on your way then," Nate said, tilting the latch and sliding it free. "This one's kind of got a jimmy to it. Dad always said he'd fix it, but we just didn't ever quite get to that."

The man rolled to his side, one hand on his collar bone and the other making a slow move toward his hip.

"I'd reconsider that," Nate said, pulling a lead rope from the pin in the saddle. "The way I see it, you're either going to get to talk, or you're going to be a body in my barn."

The man paused, then after a moment, rolled onto his stomach, putting his hands behind him. "Live to fight another day, right?"

Nate crouched over him, tying the rope around his wrists. "Don't be too sure about that. I haven't decided yet."

"You can't shoot me on the ground here. You already put one in." He grunted as Nate pulled the rope tighter. "Easy."

"Easy? As far as I know I've got every right to put one wherever I please. This ain't your land, and it sure as heck ain't your barn."

"Passin' through," the man said, his voice a mixture of arrogant laughter and genuine pain.

"I guess we'll leave that up to somebody with a star then." Nate jerked him up by the arms, sure that it hurt but not entirely concerned about it. He wanted to be alone. He wanted to get out. And this man was doing nothing more than pointing out the fact that he wasn't.

He got the would-be thief to his feet and walked him toward the barn's entrance.

"This is going to be a long night," Nate said.

"I kinda figured it'd be one way or the other." The man scoffed and it took everything Nate had to not retaliate. But for the time being, his horse was spooked, his lock was broken, and he needed to go see someone about a criminal.

Chapter Two

The horse was tired. He knew he'd ridden her farther than he should have, but if he was going to get back to Colorado, there wasn't any time to waste. Twenty miles in a day put him a good long way from where he needed to be, and it gave the Reese Gang plenty of days to get out of where he was headed.

Seven years was a long time, but some wounds didn't necessarily heal. He didn't know how he felt about going back after seven long years, but he knew he had to. Yet, it only seemed like yesterday since the old man had alerted him to the robbery at the bank; the robbery that had changed everything good in his life.

He tied the horse to a low-hanging branch. He was probably somewhere close to the panhandle of Oklahoma. Sort of back, sort of not, but at least hitting the tipping point. He gave her a long lead and went back to his makeshift camp. Twigs, bark, a few larger logs, but not enough to make the fire burn through the night. He didn't need to worry much out here. The horse would wake him if he really needed it. The problem as you worked north was the cold, but he was used to that.

What he couldn't stop, what he'd never stopped, was his mind.

Nate sat on a saddle bag, knowing he was scrunching his gear, but also not caring too terribly much. He hadn't intended to come back to Colorado, but now that he was, he knew he'd leave with blood on his hands. At least, if everything went well he would.

The man he'd yanked out of the barn seven years ago hadn't been anything other than a petty crook. He'd made his money running from town to town and staying two steps ahead of the local law. Luckily for him, the local law was typically just happy to have him move on. So when one town got tired of him, the next was ignorant of his existence. Mostly, thanks to fellows like the sheriff in Boulder Pines.

"I picked him up off the ground," Nate had said. "He was in the barn, the lock was busted. I'm not sure what you want me to say here."

"Yeah," the deputy shrugged. "But what I'm seeing is a fella with a bullet wound in the shoulder. For all I know, *his* story is the truth."

Nate bit his tongue, his father's words ringing in his ears. You don't curse, you don't disrespect women, you don't run from trouble. But the first and the last were starting to conflict in the moment.

"You think I just found this guy, shot him, and hauled him in because I had nothing better to do at one o'clock in the morning?"

"It *is* one o'clock in the morning," the man said, looking a little more offended than he should have, considering he'd taken the job. "I'm just trying to hold down the fort here. You want to talk to the sheriff, come back when he's here. Right now, for all I know, you're the one I ought to be locking up."

The man from the barn laughed. "You ought to! I was just minding my business and then…"

Nate pushed him down into a wooden chair. "Enough."

"Enough from you," the deputy said, standing up. "Now you listen, I may not be a full sheriff, but this is an office of the law. You wanna come in here and start trouble, I can take both y'all in and we can sort it out some other day."

Nate looked over at the man. In all honesty, it was impressive that he'd done so well with a through-and-through gunshot wound. His shirt was saturated, his skin was paling, but he'd kept up his attitude like it was his job.

"Whatcha think there, friend?" he used his good arm to push his hair out of his face. "From where I'm sitting, it looks like you may've just shot a fella outta nothing. Word on the street is you've been a little off-kilter since, y'know, your folks and such."

It clicked.

It wasn't the words. It wasn't the attitude. It was, as much as he hated to understand it, the fact. He was something different now.

He took a long slow breath, his glance going once to the man with the bullet wound, once to the deputy. If they wanted to treat him like he was something different, then he'd *be* something different. He squared his shoulders and looked at the deputy across the desk.

"I found this man attempting to steal a horse from my family's barn. I shot him in order to protect myself and our belongings. I'm giving him over to you to do with as you see fit."

It wasn't a grand speech, not even one that he was proud of, but he'd turned and left, because he knew any more words out of his mouth weren't going to help him.

It was his last night in Boulder Pines.

In hindsight, he regretted it. He'd stuck a note in the door frame of the family living closest to where he'd grown up, letting them know that, for all he was concerned, he was done. The place could rot. The animals, outside of the horse, were theirs to have, but he had no intention of coming back to the place that had ruined him twice in such a short amount of time.

From Boulder Pines, all he had to do was pick a direction, and for no real reason other than laziness, he headed south.

At least it'd be warmer.

He'd ridden down through the tail-end of Colorado, not really intending on a place, but knowing that every step the horse took under him was one that put him farther away from what he didn't want to think about.

Somewhere outside of Alamosa, he'd stopped for the night. The horse needed a rest; he himself was looking forward to something that resembled a real bed instead of a bedroll, and, if he was being fair, he was done with a lot of his choices.

It had been almost a week since he'd headed out and while he wasn't entirely sure it was the best choice, he was entirely sure he wasn't going to think about it. The memories hurt, the possibilities hurt; the town itself ached inside of him. He needed something new, and south was as good as anything. He climbed off his horse at the local stables, unsaddling her and giving the kid a few extra coins for a few extra grains, and he walked into town. Angry or not, a guy had to eat.

The closest place he'd seen, really the only one he'd seen, wasn't too far of a walk. But he also needed to gear up again. His backside ached and his saddle bags were empty, so the grumbling in his stomach would have to wait.

It was funny, in a way, pulling open the wooden door to the general store. He'd done it so many times before. But that was a different Nate. That one was going to work. This one was going away.

No.

That was too much.

That one was going to work. This one was doing something different.

"Watcha need there, kid?"

It was funny. Every place he stopped, it was like it was the same old man running the counter. He was surprised he'd ever gotten the job in the first place.

"Chow for the girl, mostly."

The old man laughed, pushing his sleeves up on his arms. "Where ya headed to? Cold up north, hot down south. East and west don't make much matter."

"I'm not sure." And to be fair, he wasn't, at least not in that moment. But his eyes noticed a paper pinned to the wall. "Will Bender?" He pointed to the poster. "What's the story there?"

"Ah," the clerk shook his head, rubbing the bridge of his nose. "Used to be a good kid. If I'm being honest, I'm not terribly proud of that hanging up in here like that. But…I guess you gotta let folks make their own choices."

"Meaning?"

"Well, he…" the man ran a hand through the back of his hair. "He wasn't never necessarily a bad kid, don't take it that way. But, well, let's say he got himself on the wrong side of some things."

Nate looked at the paper and back at the man. "And they're offering that much for someone to bring him in?"

"So they say, but," the man leaned over the counter, his concern almost overly evident, "you don't wanna tangle with Will. That boy'll turn you inside out before you know he's shook your hand."

Nate looked back at the paper. "For that amount of money, I think I'm willing to take the risk."

And that was how his career as a bounty hunter began.

Will Bender was barely a spot on the map in the next few years. He'd been a surprise, yes, but in hindsight, the first one should've been better thought out. You learn things though, and what Nate learned was how to make his way from Alamosa to Longwood, and do so with a heavy saddle bag of goods, and an even heavier saddle bag of greenbacks.

It was a different kind of life, one that let him keep his past behind him. He kept his family in a secret place in his mind. The Reese Gang was more of an image than a reality. Every person he tracked down, every Will Bender he tied up and wrangled toward the sheriff, it wasn't necessarily a good thing, but it wasn't a bad one either. He hadn't had any plans, but he here was.

The idea of being a bounty hunter didn't necessarily appeal to him, but he could tolerate it. It put food on the table, wherever that table might be. It kept his horse fed, which was in most ways more important. And it gave him a focus, at least for a few hours. There were still the nights, but he was learning to deal with those. The problem was the mornings. Those he hadn't quite coped with.

Of all the mornings though, this was the one he'd tried to avoid thinking about. Truth be told, any rider worth his salt would've known Nate could've made it into Boulder Pines the night before, but he'd needed a few more hours to prepare himself.

Besides, what good would riding in after sundown have done him? He could've found a room, grabbed some food and drink at the saloon, and then more than likely, laid in a bed, watching his thoughts scramble around in his mind.

No, morning was better. It was how he felt it was supposed to go.

When he made his way through the outskirts of town, nothing felt all that different. Then again, he wasn't sure what he was expecting. Certainly not a welcome wagon, and the town hadn't been bustling even when he'd left it. It was strange though, like taking a trip back in time and only he had changed.

The main street was just about the same. He recognized the mercantile, the haberdashery. The restaurant and saloon still seemed to be doing well, though in any town, those would be the two last places to die. He glanced over to his right.

Thankfully the boarding house was still there. That was usually the first to go in a dying town. If folks had no reason to pass through, it wasn't easy to keep a business like that running.

As he rode along the dirt road, something dawned on him.

He'd been away so long that this didn't necessarily feel like home anymore. He'd almost forgotten that he knew people here; that his first instinct shouldn't have been for rented lodging, but to be coming back to a familiar place. Instead, he felt a strange mix of nostalgia and separateness.

He stopped outside the local restaurant and lashed his horse to the hitching post. This was throwing him off and, after so many years of being in control, he needed some time to get his head straight.

The saloon might've been most folks' first choice. A quiet drink, decent enough food, and no one to bother you unless you were looking for trouble. But that wasn't the kind of place he needed and he knew it.

"You're grubbing next," he said, rubbing the horse's nose. "Lots to do today."

He walked up the wooden steps and into the place, only in the dimmest way aware of how travel-weary he must look. It had been a long ride, though if he were being fair, a good one. No snakes, no coyotes. No nothing, really.

But I could've used the distraction.

"Go on and sit yourself down anywhere," a female voice called.

He picked a table next to the wall, keeping his back toward it and scanning the room. If he was going to be safe anywhere, this should've been the place. But if Reese was back, he wasn't taking any chances. Then again, in his experience, most outlaws didn't get up for a morning cup of coffee. Maybe had one before bed, but noon was either the beginning of the day or the end, never the middle.

"You look like you've put some miles under ya," the girl walked over.

"A few." He took off his hat and hung it on the back of the chair next to him.

"What can I get ya? Eggs are fresh this morning."

"Anything that isn't out of a saddle bag sounds fine," he said, looking up at her for the first time.

The reaction was almost simultaneous. He knew that hair, those eyes. He'd memorized them and, other than maturing, they hadn't changed a bit.

"Nate?"

For all the tight spots he'd been in, all the bullets he'd dodged and fired, all the men he'd chased down, this was the moment he hadn't been prepared for. "It's, ah, good to see ya again, Beth." He felt stupid, but maybe he should've. You think for seven years but you never consider the fact you might run into people you knew before. "How's the, ah, how're your folks?"

"Oh, stop," she took him by the wrist.

In hindsight, it was obvious she just wanted to pull him up for a hug, but hindsight didn't help what he actually did. He jerked his arm back, scooting the chair straight into the wall and half-rising from it.

Her eyes widened. "I didn't mean anything…"

"No," he scrambled to fix his embarrassment. "You didn't do anything. I just…well, see, I've been doing some work and I'm not entirely used to that kind of thing."

"What? Touching? Or just people in general. Because, friend, there have been some rumors about you I'm dying to talk about." She smiled down at him again and for a moment he was back in the general store, waiting for her to come in, enjoying every moment of her lightheartedness, hating when she left. It wasn't quite the stomach-churning reaction he'd had as a kid, but it wasn't entirely unrelated either.

"That a fact?" he felt himself dropping into a slightly southern accent. It was probably stupid, but he needed the confidence he'd had in New Mexico, not the stumbling nerves he'd had in Colorado.

"It is, *in fact*, a fact," she grinned at him. "We've missed you around here. Word was you headed off, but where and why and what for, the answers to those questions are a dime a dozen."

He nodded. "Yeah. I reckon it was a bit of what you might call an abrupt departure."

"Most folks don't walk out on a home like you had, even if…" she hesitated, clearly realizing where her statement was about to take her.

"It's okay. I wasn't probably making choices most folks would make. Can't really say that I have been since then either, but," he held out his hands. "Here we are."

She surprised him by going quiet for a moment. Usually, Beth Ashwell was bubbly, friendly, and ready to chat with anyone about anything. But, he supposed, maybe he wasn't the only one who had changed.

She looked him up and down, taking her time. And every scar on his hands and face and neck suddenly felt all the more visible.

"Listen, I don't know what you heard," he started.

"Oh, lots of things," her smile came back. "But I think, I hope, you don't think I'm dull enough to have believed them. Or at least not all of them."

"All right," he grinned. He couldn't help himself. It was the same old Beth, just a more beautiful, confident version. "I'll bite. You tell me your worst one and I'll tell you how much truth it can carry."

"My worst?" she laughed. "I'm only the messenger. You wanna take it up with someone, we're gonna have to do some serious tracking. And don't get too cocky;

you've been gone a long time. Rumors flare up like wildfire and then just vanish out of lack of attention."

"Fair enough."

"So then at least one of the stories is right," she raised an eyebrow.

"Let's hear it."

"How about some food first, then we chat. I know I'm treating you like some kind of celebrity, but I do have other duties to attend to."

He glanced around the nearly empty dining area. "If you say so."

"Food. Then stories. Then, I have a surprise for you."

"This is starting to sound like a full day."

She glanced out the window. "That's your horse pawing at the dirt? I imagine you've got at least a few things on your agenda already."

"Nothing set in stone."

"Well, mine is. Melinda doesn't get too excited about us chatting up the clientele."

He laughed. "Doesn't sound like the woman I remember. My folks…" he caught himself. "I just was given some, shall we say, cautions about this place."

Beth smiled at him again, and again he felt that jump in his stomach. "Melinda's the same; don't worry. So I shouldn't say she doesn't like us chatting up the clientele. She just only wants us to chat them up enough to get a few extra coins out of their pockets."

Nate nodded. "Now that sounds about right."

"So you know how she'll feel if she finds out your meal is on the house."

He started to protest, but she wasn't having it. "You've been gone a long time Nate Carson. Let me give you a welcome back present. Even if it is just eggs and grits."

"Deal."

"Then you take care of that horse. Then you come find me. I'll be done by lunchtime."

"I suppose it would be disrespectful to go against a gal's wishes."

She laughed. "Depends on if it's me or Melinda."

"I try not to step on toes unless I have to."

"Well, then you're in good shape. I'll be doing the stepping this time. All you have to do is eat. You look like you've been in the saddle since the moment you left."

He nodded. She wasn't far off the mark.

And it was the best meal he'd had in almost a decade.

Chapter Three

"Oh I know my fair share of bank robbers," Nate said. "I just don't reckon they're any too pleased to know me."

The people at the table laughed and he gave them a small smile. It was strange. He knew this room, this house, this table. He'd eaten every meal there growing up. He recognized the gouges in the wood. He knew which floorboards creaked. Some things were different. The plates, the chair by the door, oddly, even the smell. But he knew this place. He used to call it home.

"So the rumors were at least partially true then?" Beth asked. "You did get wound up with some rough folks."

He looked down at the table. He was in the wrong seat. This was where his brother usually sat. "I suppose I should let the rumors fly. Doesn't hurt to have a reputation when you do what I do."

"I figured the less you were known, the better." This was Beth's uncle, Dan Ashwell. And he was also the new owner of what was previously the Carson homestead.

At least someone took it on.

"It kinda cuts both ways I suppose."

This had been Beth's surprise. She'd been nearly giddy as they'd walked the familiar path out to the edge of town, but the closer they came, the more realization dawned on Nate, he could tell she was starting to second-guess herself. But he put on a smile for the young woman. She was trying to make him happy. The unfortunate thing was, he wasn't quite sure he'd ever get back to that particular feeling again.

"So you've just been all over then?" asked Bob Ashwell, the fourth person sitting at the table. He was Beth's father and since she'd always done the shopping, he'd really only known the man to say hello to. If things had gone differently, Nate liked to think Bob would've been his father-in-law by now. But he also knew there was no sense in wondering what things could've been like. You had what you had and that was it. Wishing didn't do a darn thing.

Nate looked at Bob and shrugged. "A good many places. I don't know if I'd say all over, but the land between here and New Mexico is pretty familiar."

"Musta picked up a few tricks along the way," Uncle Dan grinned. He was clearly eating up these stories of the range, and Beth seemed enthralled as well. Bob, though, Bob seemed like he had other things on his mind. Probably some run-off, orphaned, bounty-hunter showing up with his daughter, for one.

"I'm still alive, so enough so far, I reckon."

Bob cleared his throat. "Listen, we was," he glanced at Beth as she cleared her throat, "*were* all really sorry to see you go. I can't say as I blame you, but I hope you know you ain't, *aren't* the only one that good-for-nothing Reese owes a debt to."

Nate looked up and it suddenly clicked. "Mike."

Bob nodded. "Not long after you left."

There was no accusation in the tone, but Nate felt guilt nonetheless. Mike and he had been close. It had been the way he'd finally come across Beth, actually, though at the time, she was just a girl and two rowdy boys didn't have any space in their games for her. But as they'd grown, things had changed.

That wasn't the point now though. He'd been selfish, angry, and left his best friend behind to be shot down by the same outlaws who'd stolen everything else from him.

"Sam?" Nate asked, looking around the table. This was the other Ashwell boy. They'd never been close, but he was realizing this was the closest thing to family he was probably ever going to have.

"Sam's good," Bob said. "Still at home, but it sure don't hurt to have an extra pair of hands on the ranch." He looked at Beth. "I know, I know, *doesn't*. But this type of thing *doesn't* make me feel too much worry about my pleasantries."

Beth looked out the window, seeming to barely hear her father. Nate knew the feeling well. When he'd been traveling the west and folks would ask about his family, he simply dodged it. They were up north. They were fine. He hadn't seen them in a bit. Anything to change the topic.

Apparently feeling the same way, Uncle Dan spoke up. "So, uh, what brings ya back to the Pines after all this time?"

Nate flicked his eyes to the man. "Same thing we've been talking about, I s'pose. Rumors."

Dan and Bob exchanged a glance and Beth stood up, walking to the window now, but not leaving the room. She wanted to hear what was said, clearly, but she didn't seem to have much interest in watching it happen.

"We was kinda hoping you'd say that," Uncle Dan said. "Because I think you might be more of a godsend than you realize just now."

Nate raised an eyebrow. "So they're back." It was more statement than question.

Just a confirmation of what he'd been hearing, but now at least from the mouth of a man who had a right to speak.

"Back and dirtier'n ever," Dan said. "A'course everybody talks about runnin' 'em out, but every time talk springs up, bullets start flying. And look, I like this here town as much as the next fella. I ain't got no plans on going anywhere else, especially not at this age."

Nate smiled slightly. Dan was barely past middle-age, but he seemed to enjoy the persona of the haggard old rancher.

"But I don't see what good there is in them Reese boys keepin' up like they are. You'd think they'da bled the town dry by now. But they seem to have some kind of…oh…like a pattern maybe. They come in, raise hell," he glanced at Beth, "pardon me. They come in and cause trouble and then disappear for a bit. Sheriff's acting like it's just a thing we gotta get used to. But, well, I think all of us sitting here ain't got too used to it much."

"If it makes you feel any better," Nate said, knowing that it wouldn't, "this isn't the only town. I haven't been able to quite track it yet, but I'm pretty sure Reese is just working a circuit, so to speak. The pattern, like you said. They loop around. Boulder Pines just happens to be a stop on the trail."

"So you really did come back for them?" It was Beth, her back still toward them, and her voice a strange mixture of hope and what almost sounded like disappointment.

Nate considered his answer and, once he'd said it, wasn't quite sure if he'd chosen correctly. "That's my job."

There was a slight huff from the young lady, but Uncle Dan jumped in before Nate could think about it too long.

"Well here's the thing, and I'm not trying to bring up bad blood or nothin', but…um…story goes you and Deputy Rollins didn't leave on exactly good terms."

Nate tapped his fingers on the table. It was another memory he'd tried to avoid. "I reckon that's safe to say."

"You probably don't wanna hear this, but you probably will sooner or later anyway. That fella you brung in, he walked out quick enough to have gotten your dust on his boots."

The words stung, but Nate was used to ignoring the pain at this point. "And you're thinking that's why there isn't any more trouble for the Reese Gang other than the ride."

Bob folded his hands and leaned on the table. "That's a problem we aren't necessarily concerned about at the moment. Seems to me it's something that won't bring us anything but more trouble. If you want my honest opinion, though, we've been thinking this Reese situation is one we're just going to have to solve ourselves."

Nate crossed a leg over his knee. He'd seen this a thousand times. Shoot, he'd been this person when he first decided to go after

Will Bender. But it was also different. He was alone. These people still had kin.

"You're sure about what you're saying?" he looked over at Beth's back, the gaze pointed and purposeful.

Bob's eyes flitted that way, but only for the briefest of moments. "That's exactly why."

"Listen, we know we ain't no bounty hunters like you," Uncle Dan said. "But a gang against one fella…I don't like them odds. And that's coming from a guy who sits at the faro table most nights." He smiled, but it was a weak one.

Nate sat for a moment and then leaned forward and grabbed his hat. It was the same one he'd worn since he'd left, the same one that used to hang on the peg where Dan's duster now hung. It had seen dust and blood and hundreds of miles. It was his hat, the hat of a man who knew what he was doing. These men, as much as he respected them, were just angry ranchers. It was a justifiable outlook, but milking cows and gathering eggs was a tad different than shooting a man in the heart.

He looked over at Beth, surprised to see her gaze settled squarely on him, her eyes both stern and pleading.

"All right," Nate stood up and walked to the door. "I'll think about it."

He hated leaving the Ashwells like that, but he also had a visceral reaction to the idea of putting more people in harm's way. Sure, Dan had a point. One against many was never ideal, but it also wasn't the first time he'd gone down that path. Dan also wasn't considering the risk and potential trouble he and Bob and Sam could cause. It wasn't just about having more guns; it was about knowing how to use them. For all Nate knew, the Ashwells were as likely to shoot themselves as anyone else. Sitting ducks might be good for hunting, and they might theoretically draw fire away from Nate, but that wasn't a sacrifice he was willing to consider.

He needed to clear his head, and now that he'd gone to the restaurant once, it only left the saloon. The warm beer and spirits had never been his favorite, but some acceptable food and, even more so, the numbing chatter and dim lights held a certain appeal.

He stopped by the stables to check on his horse, and then sauntered down the main drag, his hat brim down and head low. He wasn't sure how many people would recognize him, and Beth had been what might be called a special case, but it also had taken her less than a minute to place him. That wasn't what he needed.

He walked into the saloon and found a table in one of the darker corners. Here, "pleasantries" as Bob would've called them, weren't quite so important. For all the flack he'd heard about Melinda over the years, she ran a tight ship, and manners were top priority. But in the saloon, he could keep his hat on and his face shaded.

He ordered a coffee and some grub from the girl, not bothering to look up. Then he waited.

He hadn't been entirely honest with the Ashwells. Yes, the Leon Reese Gang seemed to have a pretty set circuit. And yes, Boulder Pines was on the line. But he hadn't spent seven years running back and forth between Colorado and New Mexico to come up empty-handed. The bounty hunting served two purposes. One was to keep food coming in for him and his horse. The other was to get information. It hadn't always panned out, in either case, really, but he'd been able to figure out enough.

It was no coincidence he was back now. Leon Reese should be in the area as well. At least he would be if he was keeping to his time table. And most folks, when you get them in a rhythm, it's easier to just stay there than try to change it. The question was, where was he?

Nate had been able to figure out the general plan the gang seemed to have, but knowing an area wasn't as helpful as it would seem. Colorado was sprawling and the places in between there and Longwood even more so. You could chase a man for months and miss him by a day. He could be a quarter-mile away and you'd never know it in the vast expanse of the unsettled land. Here at least, Nate felt like he had the greatest advantage. Yes, Reese had become familiar with the town. He had to if he was going to have the success he had.

But he wasn't a native son. That was the one thing Nate had that the gang didn't. He'd grown up here. He and Mike had run the place ragged over the years. There weren't many hidey-holes he and Mike hadn't either discovered or created themselves. Now it was just a matter of figuring out which made the most sense.

He sipped his coffee and drummed his fingers on the table. There were the mines out east and, despite what he'd been told his entire childhood, they'd always seemed safer than his father had let on. But that might not necessarily be a concern for a group of men who made their living shooting folks and robbing banks.

To the west was mostly tree line. It would be a reasonable place to make camp if you weren't trying to hide anything, but campfire smoke was hard to hide, and there wasn't really any way to protect yourself. The woods were a gamble no matter what. If you knew no one would stumble across you, you'd be fine, but he and Mike had spent enough time running through there to know the sightlines weren't as bad as you'd think. A group of men, a group of what would likely be rowdy, loud, drunk men, would be noticed from a good distance. Maybe they didn't care, but he also knew you didn't last long as an outlaw if you weren't good at getting attention when you wanted it and dodging it the rest of the time.

They could've gone down to the gulley, he supposed, or up north toward the foothills and mountains. But the gulley provided the same problems as the forest and even if it were just the foothills, the ride would be dangerous. Too much open land between the town and wherever the camp would be.

Then again, if you had the sheriff in your pocket, maybe you didn't worry so much about being pursued after the crime. You just needed to make your payment to the constable and let them deal with the rest.

Not for the first time, he wondered about what he'd gotten himself into. Not just with the job, but life in general. If this was the kind of thing he was trying to figure out on his own, what was the point? It was like trying to catch rain drops to keep the land dry.

The girl brought his food and he hunched over the plate, cutting the tough steak and letting his mind reel. All of his ideas felt wrong, but at the same time, almost right.

Then he heard it.

It wasn't anything of real significance, and the heavy-set, bearded, and clearly drunk man probably would never know the impact of his words. But they cut through the air like a Bowie knife and as soon as they hit Nate's ears, he knew there was only one solution to the problem.

"Yeah, well, now, ya see, that woulda been back, ooooh, thirty-some years ago," the man leaned back in his chair, looking dangerously close to tipping over. His companion, and almost comically skinny young man, who was doing his best to grow a beard and failing miserably, looked like he was only half-interested in the story, or maybe just half-awake.

"You'll see," the man continued. "You get out this way and you got a pocket full of big dreams and plans. Then you spend some time and it starts to beat you down. You gird your loins back up, but then it comes at you twice as hard. And I heard the stories, just like you did," he took a long swallow of his beer, wiping his mouth with the sleeve of his shirt. "But I tell ya, that's all they end up being. Just stories. Some fella hits it rich and you think, well, hey, why not me too? But the fact is…" he leaned across the table and hit the young man on the shoulder, bringing him out of his reverie. "I said, the fact of the thing is, if you heard somebody struck it rich, you may as well just skip that place. It's panned out. Exactly what happened to me in the Grove."

Nate's eyes flicked over.

"Yeah," the kid said, his cheek resting on his hand and his eyelids drooping.

"I spent me a good couple years," the heavyset man belched, "well, months anyway, out there at Gold Creek and I tell ya, they might call it that, but it wasn't nothin' but dirty water and a sore back for this old fella."

Gold Creek Mine. Harrison Grove.

No wonder his brain wouldn't turn off. He'd had all the pieces, just not in the right order. How he had missed it, he'd never know, but he also didn't care. If there was one place, one perfect place for Leon Reese and his men to hole up, that was it. The mine had been dead since before Nate was born, probably before his father had even gotten to town, which, he thought, made this man's story even more ridiculous. But that didn't matter. What did was that it was almost a footnote in town lore. No one went there because, what was the use? It was close, but not too close. Safe. Easily defendable. Shelter from weather and most of all, nearly forgotten.

Of course, his mind immediately went to the problems. And they were numerous. Namely, all the things that made it an excellent hideout made it the last place he'd want to chase down a group of murderers.

Then again, as he'd told the Ashwells, that was his job.

Except now it was more than that. Now he'd do it for free. He just wanted to see the blood run.

He tossed some coins on the table and left his food half-eaten, his coffee half-drunk, and headed toward the door.

***

"You sure about that?" Uncle Dan asked. "I mean, I suppose it makes sense, but I don't know if I'd want to go guns blazing at a place like that. I mean, alls they got to do is hang back and pick us off."

"That's why I'm only telling you," Nate said. "You let Bob and Sam finish their chores tonight. Let Beth do her work around the house or down at Melinda's tomorrow. But you boys said you wanted in and, the fact is, I don't know that there's anybody else in this town I feel like trusting just now."

"Well that ain't necessarily…" Dan looked up at the ceiling. "Okay, okay, I see your point."

"See it well, then. I walked out of this town with no intention of coming back, and I did the same to you earlier today. But that ain't right. You lost just like I lost and if y'all are wanting to set things right, I suppose it ain't my place to tell you otherwise. But you gotta keep this under your hat till I get back, all right? It may turn out this whole thing is a wash, or I'm just plain wrong, but I'm telling you just in case…" he stuck his hands in his pockets.

The two men were standing on the front of Uncle Dan's house, Nate's old home, and the sun was setting in a spectacular display of oranges and purples. It was something Nate had always taken for granted. *Like a foolish kid*, he thought. But the house was built at the perfect angle to the landscape. It gave you the feeling nothing could go wrong. *Till it does*.

"Beth really missed you," Dan said, putting a hand on Nate's shoulder.

The bounty hunter startled at the touch, but kept his own hands calm.

"And that's why I'm telling you. I'm not about to disappear on you all again, but I also can't stop this chase. I'll check out the place tonight and then make a decision about what to do after."

"I'm sure you'll do the right thing. You got that reputation after all," Dan gave him an uncertain smile.

"Reputations don't stop bullets," Nate said, looking off in the distance. "For now, you just hold onto what I'm telling you. If I don't come back tomorrow morning, then you can do with it what you will."

"You'll be back," Dan said. "You already proved that."

"Yeah," Nate sighed. "I'm starting to see how you can sit at the faro table every night. The odds don't mean much to you, do they?"

Dan looked at him for a moment and then broke into a genuine grin. "I guess I figure the right things have a way of happening."

Nate nodded slowly. "I suppose, in the next couple days, we'll be finding that out."

Chapter Four

He supposed it was foolish. Not just the plan, but the idea of even involving the Ashwells at all. If he went out and something happened, then so be it. Maybe it was just being back in Boulder Pines, even for the short time it had been, that was having an effect on him. He tried to shake the feeling as he mounted up and rode toward Harrison Grove, but something was different here. And it had been less than a day.

He scoffed at himself. Less than one day, just a few hours around Beth, a bit of time in his old home, and the last seven years were altering. Maybe it would turn out to be for the best, but he was keeping Dan's comments in mind. Odds were finicky, ever-changing. Just because something should happen never meant it would. And that was the only thing that was always true.

For the moment, he was just happy to have something else to focus on.

Nate had gone back into town after talking to Dan, gotten himself a room at the boarding house, and settled in for a bit of a wait. No two outlaws were the same, but there were patterns. Heading out too early would almost definitely cause him problems. Waiting too long and who knew what the men would be up to?

Assuming they're even at the mine, he reminded himself.

But something about it felt inevitable. Where else could they be?

He took the time to clean his guns, slowly disassembling them, wiping down each part, running the bore brush through the barrel, and meticulously putting each piece back in place. He'd done it hundreds, thousands of times, but it was a monotonous and predictable task. It both calmed him and got his nerves up. This meant he was being smart, but this also meant something was most likely going to happen.

Around midnight, he'd been long finished with his task and simply had been sitting on the small bed, watching the kerosene lamp burn, his hands steepled in front of him. This should be a simple task, but that was usually what caused the most trouble--the assumption of simplicity.

***

Well, yeah, course they tell you that. He could hear Mike's voice in his mind as he rode toward the mines. It was just like riding into town. Everything seemed somehow different and the same all at once.

Didn't you figure it out yet? Any place your pa tells you not to go, that's the best place to be!

In spite of the gravity of the current situation, Nate found himself smiling. Mike wasn't a bad kid, not a bad influence. He was just a kid and, as Nate had heard his own mother say more than once, boys will be boys. You can't talk about a mysterious, possibly dangerous place without a couple of nine-year-olds making a bee-line for it.

It was the same with the treehouse they'd tried to build. Though, Nate recalled, that one had been a little more than risky.

The mines, though… In hindsight, maybe their folks had been right. They were dark, unsteady, the tunnels branching off and leaving anyone without a lantern in a dark place as black as four midnights. Naturally, that never occurred to either him or Mike when they'd been "exploring," the fancy, generic term they'd given to any of their gallivanting runs around the outskirts of town.

He wondered how many hours he'd wasted; how many chores they'd left to someone else, simply because they got carried away. And yes, there'd be scoldings and reprimands, but now, looking back, he wondered how upset their parents had really been. Like Bob had said about Sam, there was always use for an extra set of hands on any homestead, but he and Mike had had the run of the town. The only one who seemed truly angry was Beth, but that was just because she was being left out.

It was ironic, in a way, he thought, bringing himself back to reality. The one thing they were told not to do would be the one thing that made this ridiculous, dangerous, gallivanting adventure even slightly plausible.

The Reese Gang likely knew the entrance to the mines, maybe a few yards back in. But they'd only been using them for a few years. Nate had known them for a lifetime.

He left his horse lashed to a tree about a hundred yards out from where the spill of overburden began. It was probably pointless, considering he could already hear the raucous laughter of the men ahead of him, but he was used to not taking any more chances than he needed to. The air smelled of wood smoke and within a few moments, he could see the dancing flames ahead.

Gold Creek Mine was a curious place. It had begun, as the fellow in the saloon had said, as one man's lucky break. But once word got out, and before everyone truly began to believe it was dry, dozens of men had come out and attempted to ply their sweaty, tiresome, and ultimately pointless trade. With that in mind, the hillside ahead of Nate was pock-marked. Some of the shafts had collapsed with time; some had collapsed almost immediately.

It was a story both he and Mike had heard individually, and the details varied just enough that, as an adult, Nate tended toward not believing it. Then again, it wasn't exactly uncommon for a miner to lose his life in his tunnel. Even just before Nate had left he'd heard kids passing along the haunted mine tales, daring one another to go at night.

But ghosts weren't particularly the problem with the situation. The spill was. It had settled around the creek and dribbled into the shafts which had slowly made their own veins in the hillside when someone had dug too close to the surface. So it was uneven. Worse, it was loud.

The good news was he didn't need to get too close. Not tonight at least.

Nate picked his way through the barest places, keeping his eyes away from the campfire in order to preserve what little night-vision he could muster. Listening had been more than enough on plenty of occasions and while he didn't imagine the Reese Gang was expecting any trouble, or at least not any they weren't confident they could handle, Nate didn't have any interest in letting them know he was there.

He'd come up from the south and picked his way toward the creek bed. It wasn't much more than a trickle these days, he saw, perhaps, the biggest difference in anything he'd noticed so far. But the softer dirt would muffle his steps, then he just needed to see a few things.

"And that gal down in the panhandle!" the voice was crisp and clear for a moment, then muffled again by laughter.

Nate waited, stock still by the water.

Mumbles, then, "...and she *still* waits for me!" More laughter.

Nate rubbed his jaw absently, his mind going cold. Whatever they were talking about, it didn't matter. What was clear was that these were men who needed to be taken down. *And not taken in*, he thought. This was no longer a dead or alive situation. He wanted them dead. Every single one. And there wasn't a drop of remorse in his heart about that.

He held up a hand, shielding the flicker of the campfire from his eyes, and counted the shafts that were still open. The number seemed wrong, but in the moment that didn't matter. If he could just remember it, he could draw it. And if he could draw it, perhaps one of the Ashwells, Sam most likely, would be able to help him piece things together. It was a long shot, and probably more risky than his father would've ever imagined the mines to be, but it was the best shot he had.

He double-checked his count, noted the position of the fire and crept back down the creek bed toward his horse. The woman at the boarding house would have a piece of paper and a pencil, surely. After that, he needed time to think.

***

The next morning, he sat back at his old kitchen table, still in the wrong chair, but surrounded by the Ashwells, Sam included this time.

"And you're sure about this?" Bob asked.

From anyone else, it would've been the one thing Nate didn't want to hear. Any uncertainty caused problems, usually at the most crucial moment. It was why he'd tended to work alone. At least that way, there was only one person to blame. But from Bob Ashwell, his face tired, but showing traces of barely hidden anger, Nate knew the question came from somewhere else. This was a nervous question, it was an anticipatory one. Bob wanted this to work and was afraid it might just be too good to be true.

"Sure as I can be. But I've been away for a while." Nate turned the rough sketch to Sam. "What does it look like to you?"

"Aw, shoot, Nate. I probably ain't been out there since you last were. I recall this one and this one here. I thought there used to be…" his finger traced up along the page.

"Okay, good. I did too. So we're missing a shaft here and here," he tapped the paper. "That changes things a bit, but remember, we're not going in, we're just trying to guess where they could come out. For all we know, if they run back with their guns firing, nature might take care of the problem for us."

"Imagine the ghost stories after that," Sam said, though no one smiled.

"You're treating them like prairie dogs," Beth leaned over her brother's shoulder.

"That's the plan," Nate glanced up at her. "The problem with a mine is, even if you can protect three of your sides, you only have one way in and one way out. Gold Creek was a little more complicated when Mike and I used to go." He looked over to Bob. "Sorry about that, by the way. I know you didn't want us over that way."

"Son, if this works, consider yourself forgiven."

"The thing you gotta keep in mind is, some of these connect. Or at least they used to. Last I heard, Reese was riding with six other fellas. That puts us at four against seven, but we're going to have the advantage of the angles. They're going to have a bit of the advantage of surprise, but we might be able to balance that out as well."

"Five against seven."

Nate looked up, but before he could say anything, Bob took the words out of his mouth. "Absolutely not."

Beth straightened up, her eyes burning like Reese's fire the night before. "And why not, exactly? I can shoot at least as well as any one of you."

"Because I said so."

Her mouth dropped open. "I'm not a little girl. You can't just order me around."

"I can and I am. You got cards in this game, ain't none of us denying that. But I'm not losing another child to this piece of trash."

"You're taking Sam."

"Beth, don't." Nate didn't have any intention of getting involved with people again, let alone a family as close to his own as the Ashwells were, but the words were out of his mouth before he realized he was going to say them.

All eyes turned to him. "This is…" he trailed off.

"Men's business?" she scoffed. "I can ride, I can shoot, and I guarantee you I'm every bit as angry as the rest of you."

"That's why," Nate said. "People think I ride out spitting nails and breathing fire. The only reason I'm alive is that I don't." He looked at the rest of the group. "And that's something you all need to get comfortable with real quick. Anger is good. It can help. It can get you through some things. But it also makes you take risks you oughtn't. It makes you dangerous, but it makes you dangerous to yourself as well. I reckon I shoulda said this before, but any of you that's heading out there looking to saunter up to Leon Reese and show him how big and bad and angry you are, you ain't riding out. All that'll get you is a bullet in the head before you see him draw."

The room was silent for a moment. To be fair, Nate had surprised even himself. It was the longest speech he'd made in, well, probably seven years. But they were things that needed to be said, things he'd learned the hard way. And he wasn't about to risk what little semblance of a family he had left. Let alone Beth.

"I don't mean to tell you you can't be mad," he said, trying to bring the conversation back. "But you gotta be able to leave it here. Once we ride out, we don't feel nothing anymore. We think, we act, and we shoot. Anything else and you may as well let me put you down right here."

"Nate!"

"Beth," Dan's voice was low and, for once, gravely serious. "You don't tell the doc what to do. You don't tell the apothecary what to do. Let this man tell us how he does his job and listen. I see some good ranchers here, but only one fella who's done this particular type of work before."

She folded her arms and Nate could see the muscles in her jaw clench, but she kept silent. And in that moment, he almost wished he could take her with him. She was right. She could ride and shoot, and in that moment, she was showing the exact type of grit a body needed to pull this off. And he almost told her, but Bob spoke up.

"Let's put all this to the side then. If we're cold, we're cold," he looked at Beth, "and we can talk about it when we get back. I can't promise you I'm not gonna have a lot of hate in my heart, Lord forgive, but far as I'm concerned, you're the boss here, Nate. When do you want to do this?"

Nate took a slow breath and folded the paper, tucking it in his pocket. This was the question he'd been dreading all along.

"Well," he said. "Now, I reckon."

It had been the thing he'd struggled with more than anything else in his night of planning. He knew the Ashwells were an unknown. He knew they'd be fired up, of course. Everyone got excited when the plan was being made. But not everyone had what it took to carry the plan out.

For a bit, he'd considered filling them in and then just ducking out, taking care of things himself. It wouldn't be the best of scenarios; especially not after having seen the mines, but it would keep them safe and give him less to worry about.

But there was also a part of him that knew more guns could be a good thing. Even if Bob and Dan just fired straight up, it would give the appearance of a larger group instead of one man. A lone bounty hunter would look like a bunny to the pack of wolves the Reese Gang could be. And to be fair, he was good. He'd held his own before and figured if he had to, he'd do it again. Or at least he'd keep trying until he couldn't do it anymore.

It wasn't right, though. Something in his blasted heart wouldn't let him cut them out. So the only solution was to move fast.

In a way, it was the exact same plan he'd hatched for Leon Reese. Show up, surprise them, overwhelm them, don't give them time to think. Be there and be done before anyone really knew what happened. At least, that was the idea. Plan at breakfast, be home by lunch; let them think whatever they wanted to think during dinner.

Bob sidled his horse up next to Nate as they rode out of town. "Y'know, I always liked you and your family."

Nate started to respond, but Bob Ashwell held up a hand. "This ain't about me feeling bad for you or telling you how sorry I am. I s'pose you've heard about enough of that for one lifetime. What I want to say, considering this may be our last moseyin' chat," he laughed tiredly, "is that back then, I admired the hell outta you. You took some hard hits, and I'm not even sure I wanna know what you been through since you been gone. But, good Lord, Nathan. You've become one very respectable man."

The words were kind, unexpected. For a moment, Nate even felt a little proud of himself. And then he realized, they were the exact opposite of what he needed. He knew Bob intended well, but there were rules to survive out here. No emotions being the first. He opened his mouth to respond, then closed it again.

"I just thought you oughtta know," Bob said.

Nate found his response. "We'll talk about it when we get back." It felt disrespectful, but it had to be done. He spurred his horse lightly on the flanks and moved back to the front of the line, effectively ending the conversation.

***

They tied off their mounts not far from where Nate had the night before. He knelt down with the other three and grabbed a dry stick from the ground, recreating his sketch of the mines in the dirt before them.

"We need to make ourselves look bigger than we are," he dug the end of the stick in the dirt. It was more of an anxious gesture than he wanted to display, but he hoped it looked like he was just defining the spots they needed to see.

"The campfire was here," he put an X in the dirt. "We got overburden like your ranch has cow dung all over." He made some lines.

Dan let out a nervous titter. "Just as slick too, I bet."

Nate looked at him. "That's exactly why I'm explaining it to you that way. You mind your footing. We aren't coming in here as a posse. We're coming in here as one bounty hunter and some fellas who tagged along. You fall, I can't come save you. You knock a slide of shale down and give us up before we're ready to go, we're all at risk. This ain't no joke now. We're here." He paused. "Which I suppose is the time to tell ya, anybody who wants to stay back, stay back. Probably be good if one of us gets out alive."

"You really got a way of encouragin' folks," Sam said.

"I'm not here to make you feel happy," Nate said. "I'm here for them." He hitched a thumb over his shoulder and looked at the three men in front of him. "Clear?"

The response was silent nods, and for the first time, Nate started to feel like maybe this would work after all.

"Who's the best shot?"

"You mean accurate or fast?"

Nate looked over at Sam. "Well, Sam, I suppose I'd prefer both but it sounds like we're working with what we got here."

"Dan's the steadiest," Bob cut in. "Takes him a minute, but he darn near never misses. Sam'd be fastest, I reckon. And I suppose I'm somewhere in the middle."

Nate looked down at the sketch in the dirt, then up at the sky. He knew the state the men seemed to be in when he'd snuck over the previous night. He also knew a drunk outlaw wasn't necessarily going to feel it the next day like your average ranch hand. The sun wasn't even considering hitting high noon yet, but this was the sweet spot in bounty hunting, those midmorning hours when your target was groggy. Not dead asleep, that could cause more problems. Not noon either. Sun was too warm then this time of year; they'd be waking up. You wanted them just in that twilight state where the first thing they'd feel was confusion, not panic.

If they were going to do this, they needed to get moving.

"All right," he poked the sketch, putting more dots in the dirt. "Sam, you know this place about as well as anybody."

There were a few more laughs and he looked up again, exasperated.

"Son, you think we ain't all been out here a time or two?" Bob asked.

Nate sniffed. "Fair enough. But it may've changed a bit since you last saw it. So like I was saying, Sam, you're gonna head this way," he pointed to the northern most mark in the dirt. "Me and your brother had a fort out there. You remember that?"

Sam nodded and, thankfully, said nothing. It was a harsh way to give directions, but this wasn't a time for sympathy.

"You get up in that area. Doesn't have to be the exact spot. I'll let you judge that. Just make sure you can see the openings. You're gonna be our…" he hesitated. "Let's just say you shoot as fast as you can as soon as you need to."

He turned to Bob. "You're the opposite end. You'll have a better angle, so don't go hog-wild. Pick your shots and do your best. Ain't much of a landmark that way, but again, you boys wanted to come, so it's time to show you can do this. I reckon there's been a deer or three who regretted being in the right place at the wrong time. You're hunting now."

The metaphor was a little too apt, perhaps, as when he looked back at Dan, the man had paled a bit.

"Uncle Dan," the moniker felt both strange and completely normal to say out loud, "you stick with me. Because I mean all that in every way you can darn well think of. They don't call it bounty hunting for nothing. We got seven murderers sitting over there and ain't nobody gonna do anything about it but us, it would appear. Me and you are cutting up the middle. I'm gonna head off a bit to the right, you stay left, find yourself some good cover and do what you do." He paused. "And I don't mean joke around."

It was a toss-off comment almost, but the other three seemed to relax their shoulders. Even a couple of wry grins.

"I'll say it again," Nate said. "These are targets. These are deer. We aren't bringin' these fellas in alive unless we have to. Even then, we might reconsider. But this has gone beyond the law. It's the code now."

He smeared the drawing out of the dirt and stood up.

"How do we know when to…?" Sam started.

"Oh, you'll know," Nate said. "Now get. We promised we'd be back for lunch."

Before he could see the looks on their faces, which he was almost entirely sure were a mix of doubt and anger, Nate turned and headed toward his position directly across from the cave he'd seen the men in. He wished he'd brought something better than the revolvers on his hips, but hopefully the rifles Bob and Dan carried, and the gun belt Sam had slung on his hips, would be enough.

Hope was a dangerous thing to have though.

He watched Dan disappear into the timber and underbrush to his left. For all his humorous attempts, the man moved like a cat. Apparently there was a whole different side to Dan. Nate made sure to take note of it.

He glanced up at the sky. Ten minutes ought to be more than enough. Judging by the sun wasn't the best way to go about things, but it was what he had.

He crouched down, counting in his head. This was yet another reason why he worked alone. He waited for the tell-tale crack of a branch and the slide of scree to form its own pile. He unholstered his gun and tapped the barrel on a fallen tree in front of him. At least it was about to be over, one way or another. He just hoped…

No. Hope was dangerous.

The sun hit its point, Nate hit his number, and he stood up, bold and clear in the midmorning light.

"Leon Reese," he called across the short space. "I'm here on behalf of the United States government, and I'm here to bring you in."

And his words were met with nothing but their own echo.

Gold Creek Mine was silent.

Chapter Five

They couldn't have—

It was all the farther Nate got in the thought before the bullets began to fly.

At first he assumed the Ashwells had gotten trigger-happy. It wouldn't have been unreasonable, even if it was not preferable. But when the rocks kicked up by his boots and he saw the muzzle flash directly across from him, he knew that things had gone, unfortunately, exactly as he'd expected.

He raced back for cover, almost pointlessly calling "Now!" as he ran.

Nate dove behind the tree trunk he'd hunkered behind moments before and lay flat on the ground. Leon Reese knew he was there, as did the other six in his posse, but they didn't know if he was bold, or stupid enough to come alone. As Bob, Dan, and Sam opened fire, he hoped the surprise of it all would turn the tables in his favor. Especially since the Reese Gang was, apparently, more of an early rising troop than he'd thought.

He should've come sooner.

"Shoulda, woulda, coulda," he muttered to himself, inching up and peering over the log.

If he could have done something, he would've planned for an evening interaction. Then he, at least, could've had the sun at a better angle. But there wasn't much to do about it now. Turning tail would've pretty well guaranteed four bullets, sooner or later. Leon Reese didn't seem the type to forgive an intrusion in his territory, and there weren't too many other towns around. Besides, reputations matter.

Nate watched the mineshaft openings. It was almost a ridiculous distance for a revolver. But only almost. The problem was the darkness. He was going to have to aim at flashes of light, not figures.

Then again…

He checked the angle of the shadows.

Maybe this would work out better than he thought. He and Bob were on the bad side of things, but Sam, and most importantly Dan, might have just a slight advantage of daylight.

As if confirming this theory, he saw a body tumble down the hillside, arms and legs immobile. He'd have to ask later, but it looked like Dan had just killed his first outlaw. The body slumped and rolled like a sack of potatoes.

"That's one," he said under his breath. "Six to go."

The valley echoed with shots, but as he listened to the rhythm, he realized something. Leon Reese and his boys weren't being sporadic. They were waiting to see where the aggression was coming from. They were counting them. And, contrary to his idea, they weren't moving like prairie dogs either.

He watched the muzzle flashes for a moment. They were regular, not taking the time to move from place to place like he'd imagined. The shafts had to still be open to allow for this kind of spread, or…

Nate shook his head. It was something he should've caught. It was the same thing he'd just done and something he'd heard his entire life.

Don't put all your eggs in one basket.

The shafts might not be open, but Leon Reese had the good sense to not put all his men in one shaft. Nate had been so caught up in his memories, in what he knew, what he felt, that he hadn't considered the most obvious thing. When you have a limited amount of people, put them where they'll be most useful.

Thankfully, it looked like Nate had perhaps done a slightly better job. Another body tumbled down the scree. This one had a little more life in him. He put in a good ten seconds of trying to catch himself before landing face first in the dirt and sliding to a stop. The red trail behind him seemed enough to tell Nate everything he needed to know.

The whoop he heard from Sam's direction may've been a little preemptive, but who could really tell? Besides, let the guy be excited. As long as he didn't get cocky. Then again, it *was* Sam.

To his left and right, the shots were methodical, perhaps not accurate, but the kind of firing that sounded like discipline, not like ranchers.

And now that the three of them seemed to have found their quiet, deadly space, it was time for Nate to revisit his.

He honed in on the main mineshaft, the one where the fire had been. Theoretically, that should've been Reese's. Boss-man gets the best bunk. Then he paused. If he was thinking it, Reese must have thought it as well.

He looked for the worst sleeping place, scanning over the face of the hill.

There. That one.

He kept his eye on the opening in the hillside, waiting. The shots were still being tossed back and forth, but every fourth or fifth one, he saw a muzzle flash from the shaft. The man was clever, waiting things out, not wanting to give away his position if he could let his men do the dirty work for him.

Another body came tumbling out of one mine, crumpled and rolling down the hill. A whoop went up from Bob. Then he cried out.

He didn't hesitate. He knew that sound all too well. He'd caused it on more than one occasion.

Nate ran, tossing pot shots off to his right as he went.

"Dan! It's me! I'm going for Bob!"

The man barely nodded as Nate tore through the underbrush and branches, briers sticking to his pants, thorns pulling at his hands. Shots kept ripping through the leaves and, thankfully, his men were acting like killers instead of citizens. But right now, he needed to find out how bad things had just gone.

Should've never brought them. You should've known better. This was on his watch. This was his idea. He had every chance to turn them back, and he'd chosen not to.

He swatted at a branch, dodged a fallen tree, and came to where Bob was laying prone on the ground, his shirt already covered in blood. Nate hit the ground, sliding on his knees over the fallen leaves as he holstered his weapon without even really realizing it. He skidded to a stop next to Bob and ripped the flannel shirt open, buttons flying.

The wound was…questionable. Nate jerked a handkerchief out of his pocket and immediately started applying pressure, trying to get the blood to stop pulsing out. Bob groaned but didn't seem to be anywhere close to consciousness.

"Unacceptable," Nate grunted. "You're coming back with us and that's just how it's going to be."

He leaned hard on the man. The bullet had caught him in the chest, but where exactly it had gone was impossible to say. It looked too high to be the heart, especially considering Bob wasn't a corpse yet. But a lung…? It was possible.

He felt his body go cold. It was how he'd always reacted in these situations, but this was the first time he'd not wanted to. He needed this man to live. He was already tasked with taking a young lady's father back to her with a few more holes than he'd left with. Actually…

"Be glad you're out, Bob. You aren't gonna like this."

Nate rolled the body toward himself, leaning over to check the back of the man's shirt. The flannel was ragged and bloody. Nate sighed. It was never a fun thing to deal with bullet wounds, but it was significantly less good to deal with ones where the bullet didn't come out. And this was good to know.

Without any other option, he reached into his pocket and pulled out his folding knife. "You aren't gonna like this either."

Nate tucked the collar of his own shirt in his teeth and flicked the tip of the knife through the threads, raggedly cutting the sleeve away. Then, in a quick motion, he slit the hankie down the middle. He took a deep breath, knowing what was about to come, and got to work.

He shoved a piece of the hankie into the exit wound, Bob almost immediately jerking back, even in his unconscious state. Moving quickly, deftly, Nate got the sleeve-turned-bandage underneath the man's body before letting him roll onto his back again.

"And one more."

He jammed the other piece of hankie into the entrance wound, keeping a knee on Bob's good shoulder while he made a makeshift dressing and pulled it tight. The man groaned and twisted under him, but it only made Nate pull the knot tighter. If this was going to work, and there was really barely a chance that it would, he needed it tight enough that Bob got pins and needles in his hands. Even then, there was no promise this would not get infected, go dirty, and the end would just be more drawn out.

He paused for a moment.

What was he doing?

If the man wasn't going to make it, why force his family to watch? Why not let him die a hero's death?

The shots rang out behind him, but more sporadically. And in the moment, they were hardly a thing that was breaking through his thoughts. Just sounds, like the wind in the trees or the chuffing a horse makes when it's having a good time. You don't notice them. Not really.

His mind went to his family, to that afternoon. It had been the same. A bell rang. A man spoke. And he was sure, or at least mostly sure, that there had been other people in the mercantile. But their voices had faded. They were just sounds.

A bullet cracked into a tree trunk about five feet away, splintering the bark and bringing him back to reality.

It wasn't his choice. These men probably shouldn't have come; he most certainly should not have allowed it. But that was a responsibility he'd took on. And now this was as well. It wasn't his job to decide who died where. It was his job to bring his men back.

"Dan!"

"I'm here!"

Until he heard the response, Nate didn't realize how fearful he'd become that all three of them had taken a hit at one point or another. "Get Sam! We're riding out!"

There was a pause, and Nate knew exactly what Dan was thinking. He'd thought it already. You can't ride up on Leon Reese and expect to ride out. But at this point, they had no choice. They could die trying to get home, or they could die in a pointless gunfight. They needed to move. And fast.

"I'm on it!"

Nate had never been so relieved to hear a voice. And there were no questions, no complaints, just understanding that the situation they were in was one Nate understood and one that the other three hadn't been in for even a moment before that day.

"All right, Bob," Nate grunted, pulling the man up to a sitting position. "No need to make you think this is going to get any better for a good long while. Grit your teeth, my friend."

He hooked his arms under Mr. Ashwell's, doing his best to avoid the wound but also very aware of the fact that a retreat left them in a more than vulnerable position. He hoisted the unconscious man over his shoulder, adjusted the weight, and made a bee-line in the direction that seemed most likely to be the one where the horses were. At this point, it was a bit of chaos, but away from the bullets seemed like a good choice.

Nate stumbled out of the tree line after Sam and before Dan. Bob's weight was a little more than he'd anticipated, but Nate's muscles were almost popping with sparks at this point.

They'd gotten three, but that meant three more were left. He'd failed on hitting Leon Reese, or at least he had to assume so. Now all they'd really accomplished was ticking off a bunch of men who were known for heartlessly committing murder. And on a regular schedule.

"We need to get the doc," he said, looking at Sam.

"He's…?"

"He needs the doc. Where's Dan?"

"I heard him behind me…" Sam said.

"Then we're counting on him. Help me." Nate walked toward his horse, the slowly breathing body aching in his shoulder. "He'll do what he does. Your job is to get to the doc. Now. I'll be behind you but this horse ain't going to run."

"But you…or he…" Sam looked back toward the woods.

"You all chose this," Nate said. "I tried to talk you out of it, but here we are. So let's fix our problems and gripe about it later."

Sam gave him a look. It was somewhere between disbelief and confusion. "You're just gonna run?"

"No I'm not gonna run, you gotta be—"

Thankfully, Dan came bursting out of the trees at that point, cutting off what may've been an expletive-laden comment.

"I'm gonna deal with this," Nate said. "You get going. I think you've seen we don't have a whole lot of time for chatter."

Sam glanced at him, opened his mouth, then closed it and put a foot in the stirrup. "We'll be there when you get back. Hell or high water." Sam sighed. "Just be fast." He jerked the reins around and jigged his horse toward town.

One problem solved. Or at least half-solved.

Nate looked at Dan. "This isn't going to be pretty - or fun - and you aren't going to be proud of yourself."

Dan eyed him. "What're you…?"

"We're lashing him on. Or you can let him die while we sit here and hem and haw. Could be about the same either way."

He nodded. "Show me how to tie it."

They got Bob onto the back of the horse, Nate crossed himself mentally, and told Dan to ride behind him. "This might get a little rough."

"I'll keep an eye out, but you know I'm not the best shot."

"I was talking to Bob," Nate said.

Thankfully, Sam was true to his word. By the time the two horses and three men made it back to the Ashwell property, the local doctor was already pacing the large, wrap-around porch. Slightly less thankfully, so was Beth.

Nate rode straight up to the front steps, Dan following along behind him. Sam ran down to help get Bob off the back of the horse, but the pale gray skin of the older man didn't give anyone a good feeling.

"I don't know about…" Sam started, then caught Nate's eye.

The cold look said more than any words could have.

"Let's get him inside," Sam said.

He and Nate unlashed Bob from the horse and carried him up the steps while Dan took the mounts to the barn. Beth, meanwhile, was fuming. She scurried from her father to the doctor to Nate and back around again.

"What's enough for you? Why did you let him go?" she turned from Nate to the doctor. "What are you doing? What's happening?" Back to Nate. "I can't believe you thought this was a good idea."

Nate bit his tongue. Not that long ago, she'd wanted to ride out with them. He knew it wasn't fair reasoning; she'd never been on a hunt before so she didn't know. And maybe he'd been bounty hunting too long to remember what it was like to be on the other side of things, but this was a pretty typical ending to some jobs. He'd hated it at first. Then he'd accepted it. You can't go out firing guns at outlaws and not expect someone to take someone every now and again.

"And what's wrong with your shirt?" she demanded, apparently finding any and everything to be irritated about.

He glanced down at his one bare arm and tried to come back into the moment. The voices in his head were contradictory and loud, telling him to just get out, but it was Beth. He couldn't walk away twice.

Before he said anything, she looked back at her father, laid out on the kitchen table as the doctor poked and prodded at his wounds, carefully easing the handkerchief to the side. "Oh," she whispered.

"It needed to be done," Nate said.

He watched the doctor work and, when she reached over to touch him, winced back. It wasn't a purposeful gesture, more so one of reaction. He hadn't been touched by a person in a long time, and usually the ones who did so weren't looking for any positive outcome.

"I'm sorry," she said, tucking her hair behind her ears and stepping back.

"No," he pinched the bridge of his nose. "I am. This should've never happened, Beth. I'm so, so sorry."

She took a tentative step toward him. "I know my father, Nate Carson. If you hadn't taken him, he would've followed your hoofprints." She sighed and pressed the heels of her hands to her temples. "This is supposed to be getting us toward a good situation, right?"

Nate looked at her, genuinely confused. "What do you mean?"

"We find the Reese gang. We get a little peace in town. We…I don't know. We get to go to sleep not worrying so much anymore."

Nate looked at her. The way she spoke was familiar, but it wasn't a tone that he liked. Beth was speaking like a person who'd already lost her father. "We'll find them."

"You're right," she said, a steely glint in her eye. "*We* will."

"Beth…"

"Are you going to fight me on this? When you created the situation? When you let this happen?"

He fought the urge to say anything back. She had a point, even if she was contradicting herself. What he needed to do was figure out how to handle the situation he'd created.

Same as always.

"What's your plan?" he asked.

"We…" she trailed off, seeming to rethink her own response. "Well, you're the bounty hunter. What's yours? Hopefully it's better than this one." She pointed toward the dining room table.

"Actually," the doctor broke in, saving Nate in a way he knew the man would never appreciate, "it's not as bad as it looks. An inch lower, then…well, to be frank, there would've been no point in bringing him back. But Mr. Carson worked quickly and efficiently. There's been a lot of blood lost, but the bandages, crude as they may've been, served the purpose. Miss…"

"You can call me Beth."

"Beth. This will be touch and go, but you keep your father with plenty of liquids, soups, stock, things that he can take without too much effort. Don't let him move about too much. The wound will take time to heal. A lot of time. But if you help him," he sat back in one of the dining room chairs, "I think he should pull through."

"You think?" Beth snapped.

"I hope," the man said. "I'm not God. I just try to keep his work going."

Beth looked at Nate. "We aren't finished with our chat yet."

She walked over to the doctor and began asking questions about the bandages, the best food, the best way to tend to the wounds. Nate went outside. He didn't need any more of this right now. Plus, Dan and Sam had been standing on the porch like two kids too scared to go to the schoolhouse since they'd arrived, and he figured he could at least save Beth the bother of dealing with that situation.

He walked out and leaned on the porch railing. The two men were in rocking chairs behind him. There was a bit of muttering before Dan spoke up.

"What's the…uh…what'd he say?"

"Well, Dan, the man got shot in the chest. What would you reckon?" He didn't mean to be so cold, but his heart and his head were fighting against one another. One part of him said to cut this off, kill the feelings, let it be another part of his life that just fell away, while another wanted nothing more than to hope Beth's father wouldn't be another person she had to mourn.

"I guess I reckon I'm not a doctor," Dan said from behind him. "I was just…I dunno. Askin'."

Nate rubbed his temples with his hand. It smelled like gun-powder and sweat. He shook his head. This wasn't how things were supposed to go.

"Doc says it'll be iffy," he spoke up, looking out across the prairie. "You want my opinion?"

"Well, I mean, yeah," Sam said. "This ain't really our area of expertise."

Nate folded his hands and leaned on the wooden rail. Even admitting he had an opinion was more than he usually did. The typical situation with Nate Carson was he got information, he followed through, and you went to lock-up. No more, no less. Feelings were irrelevant. Thoughts weren't important unless they pertained to the situation you were in.

He cleared his throat. "In my experience, with shots like that, he got lucky." He turned and looked at the men behind him. "And I hope you understand you two did as well. This ain't no joke. You both saw Bob in there. Coulda been either of you. Coulda been me. You want to start chasing down outlaws, you better start believing one of those bullets might click your ticker. Are we clear on that?"

The two men exchanged a glance, but having spent as much time as he had watching and trying to out think people, it wasn't the one he'd expected.

"What?" Nate asked.

"So we're coming along?" Dan asked.

Nate rubbed his forehead and realized what he'd done. "Aw, heck. Yeah. Of course. But don't go getting all…"

"Shot?" Sam said.

Nate looked at him but quickly saw how serious the question was. "Yeah. Don't go getting shot. We've put this girl through enough. I'd appreciate if you didn't make me cause her more hurt. You're family."

Sam rubbed the back of his neck. "You ain't far from it, ya know."

The three men walked into the house.

Nate looked at him unsure how to take the statement. "Well…" he looked at the floor. "I appreciate that." He glanced around. "But we got some things to do. Half them boys are running, and if they know anything, it's how to run."

"You know where they'd go?" Sam asked.

Nate shrugged. "Got guesses. It's not exactly a thing you just run off and do in an afternoon."

"Well make it quick." The voice surprised him, though it shouldn't have. "I've got dinner to cook." Beth walked into the room, hands on her hips and a look on her face like this wasn't a conversation, it was a declaration.

Nate looked across at Sam and Beth, his palms starting to sweat. This was the last thing he wanted. Just then, Dan spoke up. "What's the plan?"

Nate took a long slow breath. "All right. Here's what we do."

Chapter Six

He was at least able to convince the group to wait till morning, though it was impossible to talk Beth out of coming along. He knew she could be determined, remembered it well actually. And the thing was, it was that kind of determination that meant, if he didn't let her come with them, she'd just wait and follow along behind, putting herself in even more danger.

So, they had their dinner, going over all the details again, though Nate had to admit, tried to reiterate, that it was all speculation.

"They know we found them once," he said, taking a bite of the stew Beth had thrown together. "And that really changes things. There are a few places they could get to in this short amount of time. My guess is they aren't planning on cutting out. They'll want revenge."

"I never thought of Reese as a sentimental guy," Sam said. "Seems to me he'd just leave the bodies and get out while he was still breathing."

"And that's what I imagine he did," Nate said. "But it's not sentiment for his men that will keep him around. He can always build the gang back up. Right now he's got a pain in his pride."

"Plus the stories about how he isn't so tough after all."

"Exactly. He needs to send a message that if you go after him, he'll come back at you twice as hard."

"Are you really sure this is a good idea?" Dan asked. "Maybe we're the ones who should be laying low for a bit."

Nate started to respond, then considered what the man had said. "You've got a point. As far as Reese goes, he only knows one name, mine. More than likely, he thinks it was me and some other bounty hunters or lawmen. You all are still a mystery to him. We could try and keep it that way."

"Absolutely not," Beth chimed in. "He took your family. He's trying to take mine. And with my father laid up and healing, you're going to need another decent shot."

"Hey," Sam said.

"Oh face it," she gave him a long look. "Now's not the time to be bickering. Fact is, I shoot as well as anyone, better than most, and I'm coming. I might just be the one who saves your hide."

It wasn't meant as a joke, but Nate felt a little smile trace over his lips. She was one of a kind.

Sam held his hands up in mock-surrender. "Yes, ma'am."

"That's more like it," she pointed at him with her spoon. "So then, where are we going?"

"I've got a couple ideas," Nate reiterated. "We came in too late this time, but we knew where they were. I'd like to avoid that situation again. The problem is, we're going to have to get lucky or this could drag on forever. If we don't find them quick, they'll keep moving, and we'll be right back where we started. Except they'll probably change their pattern which means I'll have to go back and begin hunting all over again."

"You've spent enough time doing that already," Dan said. "What if we split up? Two against four isn't great, but four against seven wasn't what I'd hoped for either."

Nate shook his head immediately. "Not happening. I appreciate your guts, and I can understand where you're coming from, but you also saw how things went today. These boys shoot first and talk later, if at all. It's not that I don't trust you; it's that I don't trust them. And I've lost far too many people and years to this outlaw as it is. We stick together. If we don't find him, we keep looking."

The men at the table seemed doubtful. Only Beth had a grim set to her face. "We'll find him."

"You're awfully sure, considering we don't have much to go on."

"Of course, I'm sure. We don't have a lot of information, but we do have the best bounty hunter in the country. And I just have to wonder if Leon Reese isn't sitting awake right now, thinking that very same thing."

Nate felt a little color come into his cheeks and looked down at his bowl. "We'll do the best we can."

They finished the rest of their meal in silence, rinsing out their bowls and finding places to bed down.

"It's going to be a long day tomorrow," Nate said. "We need to be riding out with the sunrise. And we may be in the saddle for a good many hours. So rest up. We have to be sharp."

***

The next morning, Nate was pleased to see the two men already up and drinking coffee by the time he got his boots and gun belt on. He glanced at the table. "Beth?"

"Checking on her father," Dan said. "Don't worry. I'm not sure she even slept last night. Coffee was ready and waiting when I got in here."

Nate nodded. It seemed like a good sign. She was eager, but not running about like a chicken with its head cut off. She was being smart, methodical. Exactly what he needed.

"So where are we headed?" Sam asked. "You keep saying you got ideas, but I don't have the foggiest of what they are."

Nate pulled out a chair, looking out the window at the dark morning. "We go north."

"Not much up that way," Sam said. "Though I guess that's exactly why we're heading there, isn't it?"

Nate nodded. "A few abandoned farms. "But I think Reese is headed for the woods. It'll make it almost impossible to get the drop on him. And that's what I'd do if I was being hunted. Find the place that gives you the most advantage and takes the most away from the guy on your heels."

"Leon Reese is going to rue the day he ever stepped foot in this town."

The three men looked over to see Beth quietly closing the door where her father rested.

"How's he look?" Dan asked.

"Like the doctor said," she said, putting her hands in her pockets, "Lost a lot of blood, but it's clean. Sleep and soup. We're just lucky it didn't hit anything important. Doc said he'd come back throughout the day for a bit and make sure things are going all right, but as far as us sitting here staring at him, it isn't going to make much difference. Besides, the doc's wife said she'd sit with him for a few hours as well."

The three men were indeed staring, but it wasn't at the door, it was at Beth's outfit.

"What?" she looked at herself. "I don't have any intention of riding around all day in a dress. We still had some of Mike's things in a chest. I figured it seemed…appropriate. Plus, you want me trying to run around in anything other than pants and a flannel?"

Nate smiled. "Always thinking."

"And that's why he's going to rue the day. You and I, all of us, we aren't stupid. But we never chose to spend our time thinking like an outlaw. Now that he's given us a reason to, I think the odds are a little more stacked in our favor than he realizes."

"It's still four against four," Sam said. "We can't get cocky."

"Not cocky," she fired back, walking over to a small closet and opening the door. "We're smart and angry. Leon Reese might be pretty clever as well, but I'd just about bet the lackeys he's got riding with him spend most of their time pondering booze, money, and women. If they were so great, they'd have their own gangs." She looked at Nate. "Right?"

He watched as she found a cowboy hat and then strapped revolvers to her waist. Finally, she pulled out the rifle Bob had carried so recently before and slung it across her chest.

"You've got a point," Nate admitted. "Nine times out of ten you've got one fella who's the brains and the rest are just there to take orders, get in the way of bullets, and making the leader seem more impressive. But these men have been doing this a long time. You don't last out here if you're stupid."

"True," Sam said. "But think about yesterday. We killed almost half his muscle. I can't imagine it was the first time. All we know is this is the Leon Reese Gang. We don't know that it's the same group of men he started with. They could've been cycling in and out for years. We just hear his name and assume the worst."

Nate nodded. It was a good point. "Whatever the case may be, let's keep assuming the worst. I don't want us traipsing up there like this is going to be some kind of cake walk. We're smart, so we're careful. And we all need to be in agreement there."

He looked around at the hodge-podge posse he was leading into the unknown. If he could've done it without them, he would've. He might've even been able to. But these three had earned the right to be there in the same gruesome way he had. They'd lost someone important and it was time to put an end to this. Not just for these two families, but for everyone out west who'd felt the tragedy of Leon Reese riding through town.

"All right," he stood up, then glanced at a pile of saddle bags sitting by the door.

"We're assuming the worst," Beth said, "so I assumed we'd be out for a good bit. Packed some food."

He couldn't help it; he genuinely smiled. "Remind me to never get your ire up."

"When you acted like I couldn't come along, you were dangerously close, Nate Carson."

He nodded. "Well then let's get going." He looked out the window again. "We said we'd be riding by sun-up and it's about that time."

The three men strapped on their guns, grabbed their hats and saddle bags, and the four of them walked out to the barn.

It was going to be a long haul that day and Nate knew it. He kept the animals going slow, stopping often to let them drink out of small creeks and streams and graze on whatever they could find. North of town was mostly open fields, plains, fairly easy terrain for a horse that was used to working. This was almost like a vacation for the mounts; a leisurely stroll across flat ground where there was plenty to eat.

Still, he only had a guess as to where they were going and the last thing he needed was to push the animals too hard and cause even more problems.

"Y'know," Dan said, leaning on the pommel, "I guess technically, seeing as how only one of us is even legally allowed to be doing this, we're kind of like the Nate Carson Gang."

Nate rolled his eyes and heard Beth groan beside him. "Let's not get carried away."

"Think about it," Dan said, grinning. "We could just change direction and go find us some stagecoaches to rob. Nobody'd ever expect it."

Nate shook his head. "Let's focus on the task at hand."

"Well, so far that seems to just be moseying along," Dan replied. "Can't help it if my mind wanders. Besides, you know darn near everything there is to know about chasing down outlaws. Seems like you'd be the perfect one to lead us around and never get caught."

"Chasing and running are two very different things," Nate said. "That dinner we had last night would never happen again. You saw where those boys were bedding down. I'd take a roof over my head instead of an abandoned mineshaft any day."

"Just thinking," Dan said, the smile still wide on his face.

And a funny thing occurred to Nate. He was actually enjoying this. The danger was certainly there, and he couldn't say for sure what was ahead of them, but for the moment, riding along, chatting and listening to Dan try to constantly lighten the mood, he felt different, almost calm.

So many hours and days he'd been alone in the saddle, riding through empty spaces like this, his mind either racing or completely silent. He'd almost forgotten what it was like to have some companionship.

And, he realized, he'd been talking more himself.

"Okay," he said. "I'll bite. Where is the Nate Carson Gang supposed to go? I've pretty much burned everything south. We'd need to find somewhere where they didn't know who we were."

"Why not precisely south?" Dan asked. "The fact they all know you there would be our biggest asset." He held his hands up as if he had one of the large-sheet newspapers. "*Rogue Bounty Hunter Terrorizes Towns. Gang of Outlaws Unstoppable Under his Brilliant Leadership.*"

Nate let out a snort. "Why not the Dan Ashwell Gang? Make a name for yourself instead of riding my coattails. If we were switching to the other side of the law, I believe the last thing I'd want is for my name to be on your imaginary newspaper there."

"Hm…good point," Dan rode along for a moment in silence. "We may have to be the Beth Ashwell Gang then. Sorry, kid. Besides, nothing scarier than an angry gal with a gun."

Beth just shook her head. "There is one thing scarier."

"What's that?"

"The idea that you're going to keep talking all the live-long day."

Dan laughed, leaning back in the saddle. "I can't help it if I have interesting ideas."

"Speaking of ideas," Sam spoke up for the first time in a while. "I'm thinking I could do for some lunch. Anybody else? My hind-end and my stomach are telling me a little break might do us some good."

Nate looked up at the sky. It had been quite a few hours since they'd left. Sam was probably right. No use chasing down Leon Reese if none of them could walk properly by the time they got there.

"I'll second that," Dan said.

Nate looked at Beth, who seemed surprised he was even asking her opinion. She just nodded.

"All right." Nate looked ahead. "Let's head for that little grove of trees. We should be able to find a bit of kindling, or enough anyway. Chow, stretch, and then back to it. We've got a long way to go yet."

They had barely finished their beans and hardtack before the conversation died and all four of them looked up at the sky. Nate had been keeping an eye on it for a while, hoping the dark clouds would dissipate, but instead, they'd grown more ominous.

"So I guess I'm not the only one who's been dreading this for the last few hours," Dan said, looking at Nate.

He shrugged. "These things happen. It's why we've been going the way we have. But let's hurry things along a bit. I personally never was too fond of sleeping in wet clothes."

They hurriedly packed up their meager lunch, Sam throwing water and dirt onto the tiny fire they'd used and Beth expertly shoving things in saddle bags.

"I'm assuming you've got a plan here," Dan said, climbing on his horse and looking over at Nate.

"Always bits of a plan," Nate tried to joke. "Doesn't mean they're always good. But, c'mon." He stuck a boot in the stirrup and threw a leg over his horse. "There's a path up ahead that leads to an abandoned barn. The Beth Ashwell Gang just might make it in time."

He turned his horse and spurred it forward, hearing the other three do the same just behind him.

And they just barely made it. The shelter wasn't much to speak of, but it still had a barn and a cabin. Neither seemed particularly comfortable, but, as he'd said, it was better than being wet. And if you positioned yourself away from the leaky roof, you could stay at least fairly dry. They stuck the horses in the stables, propping the doors closed with whatever rocks and tools they could find lying about. The latches on the stall doors certainly weren't going to hold much longer.

Sam threw his shoulder into the front door of the house, the wood splitting where he'd hit it and breaking away where the simple lock had been. He paused for a moment. "You know, if this is abandoned, don't it seem a little odd it was locked from the inside?"

"There's a back door," Nate said, a small smile on his lips. "But I didn't want to steal your moment of glory."

Sam shook his head and was about to reply when a crack of lightening and an almost immediate roll of thunder split the sky overhead. "Looks like it was the last moment possible." He held the door back and ushered the other three inside.

The place had clearly been used since the time its original owners had headed off to wherever they went. A busted up, half-burned chair was in the fireplace. Empty food tins were scattered about.

"Mice," Beth said.

"They'll run off soon enough," Nate walked in and hung his hat on a peg by the back door.

"You seem pretty at home here."

Nate gave her a little grin. "I may've been here once or twice. You don't do what I do and not figure out where to go to get out of the rain. Or snow," he glanced at the partially burned chair. "Let's get that thing going again. We may be here for a bit."

Dan dragged the biggest pieces out of the fireplace, finding some kindling Nate had stacked in the corner, and in a few minutes, the warm glow was making the cabin feel at least a little more comfortable, if not exactly like a home.

"Y'know, it occurs to me," he said, snapping one of the dry chair legs over his knee and tossing it into the flames, "if you know about this place, and other folks obviously do as well, how'd you know we weren't running straight into Leon Reese's home for the night?"

Nate shrugged. "I didn't."

Dan scratched the back of his head. "Y'know, son, you've got a way of both giving and taking confidence all at once."

Nate nodded. "I figured by the time we got close, we'd know if they were here. I also figured if we were moving, they probably are too. Either way, we're out of the rain and I imagine that's exactly what they were after as well."

Dan sighed. "Maybe it's good you don't tell me all the plans every time."

Just then, Beth came down the stairs. "I found a few blankets in a bedroom. Not exactly the best, but if we're going to be here all night, it might help."

Sam cracked his back. "Even if we aren't going to be here all night, I think I'm gonna take advantage of the situation. Holed up may as well mean resting."

"I can get on board with that," Dan said. He glanced at Beth. "Two beds?"

She smiled. "Three actually. You've got your pick of the litter."

"Hot dang," he followed Sam to the stairs. "This ain't turning out to be such a bad thing after all."

Nate watched as the two disappeared to the second level and looked back at Beth. "Three beds. You can get some rest if you want to as well. I may just stay here. Keep an eye on the fire and the weather."

She walked over and looked out the window, where the rain was coming down in sheets. "I don't mind storms. Kind of like them actually."

He moved across the room and joined her. "I always sort of felt the same. As long as I'm watching from inside, that is."

"So," she said, her gaze only flicking toward him. "You've been here before. What else has Nate Carson been doing since he ran off on me?"

Chapter Seven

Nate might not have talked much over the past few years, but like most quiet people, it made him pay attention to the words people used when they spoke to him. And Beth's phrasing had him intrigued. Maybe there were more feelings there than he'd given her credit for. He knew how her coming into the mercantile had always lifted his spirits. Maybe that was the reason she'd always been the one to do the family shopping. Maybe she'd wanted to see him, too.

He shook the thought away. There could be no worse time than now to start getting attached, not when he was riding her straight toward the person who had ruined both their lives. Then again, the thought didn't seem to want to shake from his mind. And it wasn't like he was starting to get attached; he'd always been with Beth.

Still, though…

"Honestly," he said, "basically what you described. I've been running up and down, all around. You go where the outlaws go, which means," he gestured, "a lot of places like this."

"That had to be lonely."

He shrugged. "They say emotions are weaknesses in this business. I figured, the more alone I was, the less I had to lose. And if I ended up catching a bullet, it wasn't like there was going to be anyone upset about it."

"I would've been." She kept her gaze out the window, her voice calm and even.

Nate let out a sigh. "It's one of the reasons I left like I did. If something had happened, no one would've ever known."

"Word travels."

"Some bounty hunter dies in the New Mexico desert? They'd never find the body. I'd just be…gone."

Saying the words out loud, hearing himself, seeing her wince, he'd never considered how cold, how selfish his choices had been. He'd been overwhelmed, angry, and had acted in the way that suited him best. Maybe there was some justification to it. Maybe he hadn't thought things through. But he'd also been a teenager. Everything frustrated him and nothing made sense back then.

He shook his head. And yet he'd been ready to marry Beth if he ever got the nerve to tell her how he felt. How could he have thought himself so mature on the one hand and acted so immaturely when life got rough?

"For what it's worth, I missed this place," he said.

She finally turned, a teasing grin on her face. "It is a real humdinger. You got the holes in the roof, the mice in the food. I don't know how you could stay away."

He smiled a little. "Boulder Pines. I think one of the reasons I stayed away was that I knew, if I came back, it would be that much harder to leave."

"But you did come back."

He sighed. "Leon Reese."

"You could've picked up his trail anywhere and you know it," she nudged him with her elbow.

She was right. So why had he come…he almost thought 'home' but wasn't quite ready to make that jump. Why had he come back?

"I guess," he started, then stopped. "I s'pose I kinda wondered that myself." He could feel his heart rate pick up. In a gunfight, his hands were calm and steady. His brain was clear. But now here, talking with someone he'd known most of his life, he was a bundle of nervous energy.

"And all that time in the saddle, you never came to any conclusions? I find that hard to believe, Nate. You're too smart to not have figured it out."

He rubbed the back of his head. "I guess I figured it was some kind of justice thing," he said. "I know that's an idea that gets tossed around a lot and certainly doesn't milk the cows or gather the eggs, but my father raised me with a code. It seemed only right that, if I was going to take everything away from Reese, it should be in the place he took everything from me." The nerves calmed as he imagined it. His mind was in the gunfight already; his emotions were stilled.

He stared out the window at the storm and thought about watching the man die, about how he hoped he'd have the chance to be up close when it happened. They'd brought rifles and had a few good marksmen with them, but Nate wanted to look into Reese's eyes as the light faded out of them. He wanted to tell him who he was, why he'd chased him. He wanted the man to know he'd died the moment he shot the Carsons. It was just a matter of time.

"Nate…"

Beth's voice brought him out of his reverie.

He glanced over.

"You were somewhere else there for a moment. And, not to be a typical girl, but you looked scary. Are you all right?"

He nodded, putting in a conscious effort to unclench his jaw. "Just thinking."

She put a hand on his forearm. "I know you think you're alone. I know you've put a lot of work into keeping yourself at a distance from everyone. But just because you think you want that, it doesn't mean you're the only one who's been hurt. You lost a lot. But don't forget that I lost Mike, too. It wasn't just your family, your friend. It was my family, my brother. When you rode in with the doc and my father last night…" she put a hand to her forehead. "If Leon Reese had been there I wouldn't have shot him. I would've wrapped my hands around his throat and loved every second of watching him die."

Nate looked over at her, eyebrows up. This was certainly a side of her he'd never seen. Though, if he were being honest, somewhere in the back of his mind, he'd always had a feeling it was there. It was one of the reasons he'd always had an eye on her. She didn't mince words, she didn't back down. Be nice to Beth and she'd be twice as nice to you, but he had a strong feeling that that particular sentiment went the other way as well.

"We'll find him," he said, then nodded toward the window. "In fact, rain's letting up. Grab your uncle and brother. No sense in wasting time here."

They followed the muddy trail up through the woods, coming through the tree line to a small, but bustling town. The trail widened out in front of them, turning into what was one of two main streets in the place.

"Another one of your old secret hangouts?" Dan asked, swatting at a bug on his neck.

Nate shrugged. "Obviously it's not that secret."

"It's not exactly a boom-town either."

"It pays to know where places are," Nate said. "I did a lot of running around. Horses need food. I needed bullets."

"Wait," Sam looked around, checking the terrain. "We're not all that far from Harrison Grove."

"Nope."

Nate led his horse down to the only real intersection in town, dismounting and lashing his horse to a hitching post. "And since we're talking about food, let's take a wander about. You all find something to eat if you want. I'm going to see if a certain fella's sitting in his usual seat in the saloon."

Beth gave him a long look. "You sure you don't want some extra friends coming with you?"

Nate glanced at the door of the saloon. A hand-painted, haphazardly hung sign was tacked above the door. *The Silver Barrel.* "This place isn't exactly somewhere I'd be inclined to take my friends. Besides, I've done this a time or two."

"Well, one of them's going to be your last," she said, looking down at him from her saddle.

"Let's hope it ain't today then. There's a restaurant just catty-corner from here," he nodded toward another storefront. "Get you some coffee. Warm up a bit. If you hear a ruckus, then you'll know I might need some extra friends. So come along quick."

Dan looked around. "We're not faster than a bullet."

Nate raised an eyebrow. "You don't have to be faster than the bullet. Just faster than the other fella's hand. But I'll be all right. It's just not…" he pushed his hat back and scratched his head. "It's not what you'd call a place for decent folk."

As if on cue, a kid no more than eighteen came flying out the batwing doors, bouncing down the stairs and hitting the dirt of the road.

"Ya ain't got the money, don't take the seat!" The man standing in the doorway was huge, bald, with a handlebar mustache and a belly that must've entered rooms a good few seconds before he did. He glanced over at the quartet. "Goes for y'all as well!"

The kid got up and dusted himself off, making a bit of a staggering walk down the road, though if it was from the liquor or the toss, Nate wasn't sure. Nor was he concerned.

"Billy."

The man turned back, then walked out onto the wooden porch, shading his eyes. "Well I'll be a…" He moved as fast as his girth would let him, stepping down and pulling Nate into a bear-hug that felt like it might break his ribs. "Nate Carson! I coulda used you a minute ago."

"You seem like you did all right," Nate said, pulling back and trying to catch the breath that had just been squeezed out of him.

The man he called Billy laughed. "Yeah, but the sheriff probably would've preferred I had another lawman tossing those kids out."

"Not a lawman," Nate said.

"Close enough." The man put a hand, or what was perhaps closer to a paw, on Nate's shoulder. "What brings you back around? It's been…" he looked up. "Well, the liquor catches up with a fella. It's been a good long while."

"Too long."

"You riding with a posse now?" Billy looked over at Dan, Sam, and Beth. "Oh, I apologize, ma'am. Eyes get used to the darkness."

"Closest I've ever had to one, I guess," Nate said. "I'm sending them up Regina's way. I was hoping to cross paths with John."

"Good choice," Billy said. "Y'all ain't gonna find better food in town. And I'd know," he let out a belly laugh. "I'm the only other place that serves any. Do yourself a favor and get some grits. Old Regina's got a way with butter and pepper that just…" he patted his stomach. "Well, you can see."

Beth gave the man a long look and Nate watched her. "It's all right, Beth. With this animal on my side, what could I have to worry about?"

She gave him a sideways glance, but she and her relatives turned and rode off in the direction of the restaurant.

"That's quite the filly you got there," Billy slapped a hand on Nate's back, almost knocking him down.

"She's a lot more than you'd think," Nate said. "One of the best shots I've ever seen. And a temper for days. So let's leave her out of this. What's new here?"

Billy stopped just inside the door. "I can give you the local gossip whenever you want, but if you're looking for John Nelson, I'd recommend you get to it before he gets too far in the bottle. He's been here a good long while as it is and he ain't holding his liquor like he used to."

Nate nodded. "Usual spot?"

"Table in the corner. At least he's still trying to keep his back covered."

Nate let out a sniff of a laugh. "Like a true gambler."

"Like a true cheat," Billy said. "But he keeps getting games, so I guess the only fellas to blame are the ones dumb enough to sit down with him. Can I get you anything? It's on the house."

"Maybe in a bit," Nate said, turning toward the familiar wooden table that sat off in one of the darkest areas of the saloon. "Sounds like right now I need to get to work."

"You still tracking that Reese Gang?" Billy stepped behind the bar and pulled a dirty rag from the shelf beneath, attempting to put the tiniest of effort into cleaning a glass.

"I'm tracking everybody," Nate said. "Just like usual."

He walked over to where John Nelson was sitting, eyes half-hooded. He supposed he really was tracking everybody; any poster with Reward on the bottom was good enough to get his attention. But that didn't mean he needed to advertise his business. Talking with Nelson was a risk, but it was a calculated one. And if he was as wet-brained as Billy seemed to believe, there was a pretty solid chance the man wouldn't remember their conversation by the morning anyway.

"John," Nate sat down, snapping his fingers to get the man's attention.

Nelson looked up, bleary-eyed. "Howdy."

"Well this ain't too promising, but we need to have us a little chat."

"You're that…" Nelson pointed a shaky finger at Nate. "That fella. I 'member you. Used to come through here, stirring up…" he belched. "Stirring things up…" he waved a hand in the air then leaned heavily on the table. "How you been, partner?"

"Busy," Nate said. "But if I recall, you might be able to help me with that."

Nelson leaned back in his chair, lost his balance, but only tilted back a few inches before hitting the wall and rocking forward again. *Watching his back*, Nate thought. *I suppose there's more than one way to take that.*

Nelson grinned, showing a glaring lack of teeth since the last time Nate had seen him. "You look like you've seen better days," Nate said. "Let me get you something to eat."

"I don't need no charity," the man gave his best attempt to sound gruff.

"It's not charity. I'm buying something from you," Nate said.

"Well in that case," Nelson gave him an ornery grin, "I 'pose, I *suppose,* I'd be rude to not oblige."

Nate beckoned the saloon girl over. "Anything that has a lot of bread, some coffee, and…" he looked at Nelson.

"A steak!"

Nate sighed. Maybe it would be worth it. As long as the alcohol got soaked up he had a fighting chance. If John Nelson was as far gone as Billy seemed to think, it was probably a waste of time and money. But Nate didn't exactly have a lot of bills to pay and the reward money had been piling up a good long time.

The saloon girl looked at Nate. "And a steak," he said.

"You new in town?" she said, a hint of warning in her voice.

"Just passing through," he said, "but I've been here enough to know what I'm about to get into."

"All right, honey," she shrugged and looked at Nelson. "How you want that?"

"Bloody as can be," he tried a winning grin, but really only succeeded in showing off his poor dental hygiene and lack of sobriety. "How men eat 'em. You flop that thing down and flip it before it starts to sizzle."

Nate's stomach turned and it looked like the waitress was feeling the same. "Whatever you say. Just don't come banging back in here when you get done coughing it back up."

Nelson patted his barely existent stomach. "Like an iron kettle. Don't you worry about me, Missy Mae."

She gave Nate one last, almost sympathetic glance, and headed off to get the drunken gambler his food.

"So…" Nelson leaned forward again, one eye squinted. "You…" Both eyes darted open. "Nick! No. Ned?"

"Nate."

"That's what I said!" He leaned unsteadily over the table to pat Nate's shoulder. "Been a good long time, my friend. What can I do for ya? Lemme get ya a beer."

Nate leaned his elbows on the table and put his head in his hands. This was going to be so much more than he'd anticipated. So much for plans working out well. Then again, hope for the best, prepare for the worst. He took his hat off and rested it on his knee, running a hand through his hair.

"I'm good, John. Thanks. I just wanted to ask you a couple things."

"Ask away," Nelson said, looking for all the world like he'd just run into his long lost friend. "Been too long since we had us a good chat." He stopped abruptly. "Wait, this isn't about…" he raised his eyebrows as if Nate was supposed to have any idea what he was referring to.

"I don't know," Nate shook his head. "What do you mean?"

"You know…that certain game with that certain fella who make certain," he belched again, "accusations. Which, I just gotta say, were…uncalled for." He looked proud to have come up with the phrase.

Already running out of patience, Nate pushed ahead. "I don't keep up with your gambling, John. I didn't even have any intention of coming back to this town. But you hear things at the table. I'm looking for Leon Reese."

"Oh…oh! Well, heck. You come to the right fella. I know all kinda things. Like you said, men like to talk when they get the cards a dealin'. It ain't free though."

"Your steak's probably done by now," Nate said. "Remember?"

Nelson scratched his chin, as if trying to see whether he was being conned or not, then decided to commit. "I's just testing you. Making sure you remembered."

"It was a good play," Nate said. "So what's the word on Reese? I thought he usually came up this way every now and again."

"Funny you should ask, really. I just was hearing about him earlier today. Apparently, he's been seen poking around the edges of town. I don't know what truth there is to it, but if I were you, let's just say there is a particular place I wouldn't wanna be in today."

It was a little town in the middle of a bunch of nothing, but that didn't mean there wasn't at least some money floating around. And for someone like Reese, it made a perfect target. There wouldn't be enough official law in town to put up much of a fight, even less to put up a chase, and most folks would've just been glad to see him ride out as anything. And Nate had been here before, many a time. No vigilante justice, no desire to put up with it. People like Reese were just a part of the territory. Same as Nelson.

"He's going for the bank?" Nate asked.

Nelson shrugged. "Maybe he is, maybe he ain't. But if he does, you best make sure you didn't hear it from me."

It was the most convoluted sentence Nate had heard in a while, but it was what he needed. "When?"

Nelson shrugged again, looking sleepy. "Whenever he feels like it, I reckon. Don't believe Leon Reese keeps himself a set schedule."

Nate bit his lip. If Reese didn't keep a schedule, Nate wouldn't have made it this far. "You're sure?"

"Sure as..." Nelson yawned. "Sure as a fella can be, I s'pose. Just what I heard. And I am sure I heard it. So..." his head bobbed and he seemed to wake himself up, at least slightly. "I think I might need myself a coffee."

"It's on the way," Nate said, standing up.

"Well that's real Christian of ya, my friend."

"Don't mention it." Nate walked over to the bar, catching Billy's eye. "That fella's seen better days."

Billy shrugged. "He pays at least."

"Well, today's on me." Nate put some money on the counter. "And if I were you, you might think about adding a little more water to his beer than usual."

The bartender looked at him, mock-offended. "I would never…"

"Save you money," Nate glanced back at Nelson. "And trouble. Good to see you, Bill, but I gotta run."

"Be careful," the burly man called after him. It was his usual way of telling Nate goodbye, and every time it felt out of character for such a bear of a man. But, Nate thought as he headed out and crossed toward Regina's restaurant, maybe he just hadn't been paying attention to how many friends he had after all.

"You're kidding," Dan said, sopping up gravy with a last bite of biscuit.

"I can't say for sure. The fella I talked with wasn't…let's just say he was a little unreliable before. Now I'm not sure he even knows I was there."

"So why trust him?" Sam asked. "You said the whole point was to keep moving quick. The more time wasted, the less likely we are to track 'em down."

"That is the point," Nate said. "But we're also here. And no matter what you say about John Nelson, some things stick. He's always been that way. He listens. He remembers. Mostly because he can leverage it for gambling debts or free meals. You wanna ask him the last time he took a bath, you'll probably get nothing. But you wanna know the dirt on the town, he's usually got it."

Beth took a sip of her coffee and shrugged. "So we stake out the bank. There's four of us. Everyone takes a side and we ought to have plenty of warning."

"I was…" Nate caught himself. He was about to say 'I was thinking the same thing,' when he looked up and saw who he was talking to. "I was considering that," he changed course, "and if we were four lawmen, you'd be exactly right. But all we'd be doing is putting the odds even higher that one of us gets shot and the bank robbery goes off anyway."

"So what's your plan, then?" she asked, and he could hear the irritation already creeping into her voice, almost as if she knew the answer before she presented the question.

"You and Sam hang back," Nate said, wincing slightly at the words, and even more at the look on her face. "Not out, just back. It's been a while since I rode through here, but last I recall, the sheriff was about as likely to chase down Leon Reese as you'd be to grab a rattler by the tail. There's a mercantile across from the bank. Dan and I will spend some time there, walk the street, just kind of be around. The two of you," he reached in his pocket and pulled out some cash, "get a place at the boarding house."

She scoffed and started to protest, but he cut her off.

"You ask for the room on the corner. You can see the bank from there. Anything starts to happen, you'll have a good angle and you won't be left in the dark."

"You think I can't handle myself, after all," she said, her eyes fiery. "All this time and you just let me ride along so you can keep an eye on me, didn't you?"

"No," he said, his voice low. "I want the best shot looking over me. We put you two up high and we give ourselves an advantage. All four of us on the ground is just wasted opportunity."

She raised an eyebrow. He'd scrambled for an answer. Of course he wanted her out of harm's way. Ideally, he'd put them all up in a room away from the bullets. But he had to work with what he had.

Thankfully, she seemed to buy it. "And how long do we wait?"

He leaned back in his chair, his shoulders relaxing slightly. "Reese likes to put on a show. I'd guess he'll come around the end of the day, right when most folks are coming in to do their business. If nothing happens, I'll head back and talk with Nelson again. If he's peddling the same story for a steak, we ride out tomorrow. But we can't risk that he's right." He looked around the table. "Are we agreed?"

It was a heavy pause, and of all people, Dan, who would be sticking his neck out the farthest, spoke up first. "If that's what you think, I reckon we'd be foolish to not trust you. Ain't nobody else here done this before."

His drawl was slowly coming back, something Nate had noticed whenever Dan's nerves kicked up.

"I appreciate that, Dan. What about you two?"

Sam and Beth exchanged a glance, and she spoke for the both of them. "Like Dan said, you're the one with the experience. But I swear to you Nate Carson, if you get yourself in trouble…well, you just remember where you put the person with the best shot."

He smiled, though it was one nearly devoid of joy. "I'll remember." He looked out the window at the street as it was slowly starting to fill with folks coming into town for their errands. "And I reckon we better get a move on. No telling when this will happen."

"Or if," Dan said, sounding almost hopeful.

Nate wasn't sure if he shared that same hope or not, but he agreed. "Or if."

Chapter Eight

Nate escorted the rest of his group to the boarding house, more to make sure Beth really followed through than anything. Her attitude was curt, quiet, and he understood why. She thought she was being taken out of the action. But there was more than a little truth to what he'd told her, he realized. Reese would likely come in hard and fast, making as much of a ruckus as he could. But his men would all be with him, on the street-level. Putting Beth up where she could keep an eye on things would certainly be the best place for any sharp-shooter, man or woman.

But, having Sam there with her wasn't exactly a bad thing either. Nate needed someone close to Beth. Her brother seemed as good a choice as anyone to keep her safe and do what was needed.

Assuming the time came, he reminded himself.

The woman at the counter eyed them when they walked in, guns on hips and slung over shoulders.

"And just what do you think you're about to get up to?"

"Just passing through," Nate said. "Asking questions. Moving along." He pulled a piece of paper from his breast pocket and looked at the trio around him. "We're bounty hunters." He handed the sheet over. "Weapons are kind of the tools of the trade."

The woman adjusted her glasses and looked at the sheet, then back up at Nate. "Even her?"

"One of the best," Nate said. He saw Beth look down and blush a little out of the corner of his eye. Maybe things weren't working out so poorly after all.

"Y'all are staying here for…what? The night?"

"Possibly," Nate said, then corrected himself quickly. "Probably. We'll pay full either way. We've just had a long ride. Me and my partner," he nodded toward Dan, "are heading into town. See what we can see. These two are needing a break."

The woman still seemed skeptical, but didn't have much to argue with. "So how many rooms?"

"Well," Nate tried to put on his best, innocent, 'aw-shucks' expression. "If we can, I reckon we'd take the four you got facing the street."

The woman's eyes widened. "That's half of what I got."

"And we can pay you now," Nate said, pulling some greenbacks from his pocket. "If that's all right with you."

The woman looked at the wad of money in his hand. "Be a fool to not say yes…" she looked at the four of them again. "You're not bringing trouble in here, are you?"

"Our job is to keep trouble out," Dan jumped in, giving her a winning smile. "And if you're lucky, we'll be on our way before sundown. Just trying to plan ahead."

She hesitated a moment longer, but the money just looked too good. "All right. The four front rooms, you said?"

"Yes, ma'am, thank ya," Dan smiled again and Nate saw Beth put a hand up to her mouth, covering a smile.

"Let me get you to your quarters then."

"We'll come back for ours," Nate said, "My… associates can tend to this well enough, I reckon."

"Suit yourself, um, officer?"

"Nate's fine."

"Yes, sir." She looked at Beth and Sam. "Well it looks like you get your choice. Sun comes in pretty warm in the morning, but by then most folks are down for breakfast anyhow. Now there's a place around the corner, Regina's…" her voice trailed off as she led Sam and Beth up the stairs.

Beth gave him a long look before passing from view. It was complex, a mix of emotions. But there was something there, more than just worry over a friend. He nodded and turned to Dan, who was staring at him, a giant grin on his face.

"So…"

"Nope," Nate cut him off. "Not now. We've got work to do."

"I was gonna say, so we're partners," he scoffed, heading toward the door.

"Well in that case then, it certainly looks like it."

They headed back out and over to the mercantile.

"Ain't they gonna think it's weird, us just hanging about? Last thing we need is trouble when we're supposed to be watching the bank. Then again, last thing we need is to be standing here watching the bank…" he paused. "How do you do this?"

"Well, first, I don't stand about. We've got plenty of things we can pick up at the general store, which gives us a reason to walk back to the horses and take the horses to the stables. We're just regular folks, doing regular folks things. The only important thing is that we stay close to this area."

"I gotta say," Dan laughed, holding the door open for Nate, "I feel like I got the better end of the deal. Having something to do is better than sitting around and staring out a window any day."

"Yeah, we'll see if you change your tune when things start…" Nate glanced up and saw the shopkeeper looking at them. "When things get busy," he finished.

"Help you boys?" the old man asked.

"I reckon we can handle it," Nate said. "But if we need ya, we know where to find ya."

The man gave them a strange look, but more likely because he'd been left out of the conversation than anything. Nate and Dan strolled around the store, picking up a few random supplies for them and the horses. If the shopkeeper had been paying attention, he might've noticed that they did almost all their perusing close to the front windows, but he'd gone back to whatever paperwork he had laid out on the counter in front of him.

About thirty minutes later, Nate was beginning to feel like they'd been around long enough. He took an arm-load of things up to the counter and laid them out, Dan placing his handful next to them.

"Boys heading out on a ride it looks like," the old man said.

"Always somewhere to ride to." Nate reached in his pocket and pulled out a little more money, not unaware of Dan staring at the apparently never-ending supply of cash Nate had.

He paid quickly and got them back outside.

"I live in the saddle," he said as they walked back toward the horses. "What am I gonna do with the money? And where am I gonna keep it but with me?"

"Hey," Dan held out a hand, palm up as they crossed the street in front of the bank. "I'm not judging. Just thinking I may've picked the wrong business. I get money in, it goes right back out. Never quite had the luxury of being weighed down by the burden of my cash."

Nate laughed, shaking his head. "Ironically, it comes at a price."

Just then, the gallop of hooves tore down the street behind them and a shot rang out. Dan stumbled forward a few steps and fell, spilling his recently purchased items all across the dirt in front of him.

Nate didn't think. He only acted. It was the crack of a revolver that had become ingrained in him. His body was in motion before he realized what he was doing.

He tossed his dry goods to the side and grabbed Dan by the shirt collar, already knowing by the slump of the man's head that Leon Reese had just stolen one more person from him.

Nate made a quick run across the street, getting himself and Dan behind a rain barrel and then around the backside of one of the ramshackle buildings. He couldn't think of any reason Reese would bother following him. The bank was their goal. Shooting a random citizen on the way in was just the gang's way of showing they meant business.

He could hear the screams and running feet as he moved away from the main road, but they were far back in his mind, barely registering. He sat Dan up against the building, taking him by the chin. The skin was still warm, but the eyes were vacant. Blood poured down the man's chest, soaking his shirt and dripping out through the ragged hole over where, twenty seconds ago, Dan's heart had been beating.

Nate felt his own heart and mind shut down. This wasn't a time for sentimentality. He stood up, hand already going to his hip.

But despite the chaos he could hear on the main thoroughfare, he paused.

He knelt back down and took Dan's chin in his hand again. "This is the last time," he told the dead man. "It ends now. One way or the other, I'll be seeing you soon."

He raced back down the alley, the confusing sound of gunfire and screaming coming from every direction.

Chapter Nine

He didn't know if Beth had seen her uncle go down. He didn't really even consider the possibility. What he saw was a dead body on the porch of the bank and, when he looked back, the glint of a gun barrel sticking out of the boarding house window.

"Good girl," he muttered.

A shot splintered the wood next to him and he ducked down, looking for anywhere that would provide cover. He'd barely caught a glimpse of the men when he'd been dragging Dan out of the road, but it didn't appear there had been any more than four of them. So Reese hadn't added to his gang yet.

How could he have, really? There hadn't been enough time and…

Of course. The bank. He needed money. Hard to hire folks on just your good word. Especially if you're an outlaw to begin with.

Nate pulled both guns and held them barrels up in front of his face. They'd taken Dan, but Beth, presumably, had taken one of Reese's men. So, three on three.

He stood and turned, running around the back of the building again. Maybe Reese hadn't taken the luxury of his prairie dog moment, but Nate certainly wasn't going to let his pass by. Before he made it back to the main road though, he realized something.

Yes, shots were coming from above him, where he assumed Sam and Beth were doing their best, but it was a cacophony of shots. The three men who had come for the bank had wildly miscalculated their odds. This wasn't three against three. Maybe with a full posse Leon Reese had intimidated the town, but the numbers seemed to have shifted.

Nate ran, hunched over, toward the corner of the building. Sure enough, just down the walkway, he could see the hulking form of Billy, rifle in hand and a look of rage on his face.

"Billy!" Nate yelled. "It's me! Keep the bullets going that way!" he waved his gun barrel toward the bank.

"Gladly. I've had enough of that son of a…" the blast of his gun drown out the last word, though Nate could finish the sentence easily enough. And he couldn't think of a more fitting moniker for Leon Reese.

Nate poked his head around the corner of the building. In the brief time it had taken him to double back, another man lay dead on the wooden sidewalk. Nate hadn't seen enough of the gang to really recognize them, and the posters had always been Leon's grimacing mug, but the bandana covering the lower half of the dead man's face seemed to be indication enough.

"So you're down to two," Nate muttered. It wasn't the revenge he'd wanted, at least not in the way he'd imagined it, but he was ready to end this and he knew the how and where didn't matter in the least.

Bullets flew in the small town. The old shopkeeper, someone Nate would've never known from Adam, lay bleeding in the street, beside what looked to be a blunderbuss by his outstretched arm. In the other direction, a man's body was draped over the hitching post, lifeless arms almost swaying in the breeze. The town had finally decided to stand-up for itself, and they were paying the price.

But these were the hard choices, and even not committing to making them was a choice.

His eyes scanned the front windows of the bank. The glare of the sun made it almost impossible for him to see in. Besides, they were shapes, shadows. They could've been anyone.

A shot cracked from overhead and a window shattered, yet another man with a bandana draping out through the frame. He leaned forward, looking up at Beth who was frantically pointing toward the building, yelling something he could just barely hear over the incessant gunfire.

Then it clicked.

"The back! He went out the back!"

Nate raised a hand in understanding and turned back to the large man up the way. "Bill! There were four! Three are down!"

"Well where's the other?"

"I'll take care of him. But you're all just shooting at yourselves now and I don't wanna run through the middle of it."

Billy's voice was as large as his body and personality. "Hold your fire, for Pete's sakes! We got a bounty hunter coming through!"

There were a few lingering snaps and pops, making Nate wonder if they'd brought their .22s and bb guns to the fight. Then again, it was better than nothing. He stood and raced up the street toward the Silver Barrel where his horse was still hitched out front, where he and Dan had been trying to go before everything had gone sideways.

"Thanks, Bill," he said, shoving his guns in their holsters and practically jumping on the horse in one swift movement. "I'll be back. Meantime, get down behind the mercantile. I left a friend there and his niece doesn't need to see it."

Billy just nodded. "Whatever you need."

He rode back to the street in front of the boarding house. "Which way?" he yelled up to Beth.

"Straight out the back, then he went left. I think we got him, but he's got some skip in his step either way."

"Got it. The two of you sit tight. I ain't got time to wait." He turned his horse before she could protest. There was no question anymore. This was between him and Reese and it would be the end of the trail for one of them that day.

He spurred his horse, the animal jumping up as it put all its power into moving forward. He flipped the reins back and forth, urging her on. The dust still hung in the air from where Reese had made his cowardly escape and, while he couldn't be sure in the blur of dirt, it looked like there were some tell-tale dark droplets passing by. Maybe Beth had gotten him better than she realized.

He turned his eyes ahead and his stomach dropped. It was what he'd said all along. Yes, there was Reese a few hundred yards ahead. And just beyond that, the place the outlaw was clearly headed for was a small grove of trees.

The odds had shifted for a moment; it was going to be one on one. Now, the man was going to disappear into the trees and Nate, whether it was a good idea or not, was going to go right in after him.

He urged his horse forward, trying to close the distance as much as possible before the man could get inside and hunkered down. Reese sent a few haphazard shots back his way, but with a revolver from a galloping horse at that distance, he may as well have just tossed the shells on the ground. Nate gritted his teeth and kept his nerves cold. This was going to get better before it got worse and he'd likely need every bullet he could get his hands on.

Sure enough, it was only a minute or two before Reese disappeared into the woods ahead. Nate knew he was nothing more than a sitting duck at this point, but the longer he was out in the open and Reese was hidden in the trees, he couldn't really solve that problem. So instead, he jerked the reins, turning the horse hard to the left, reducing the angle and getting him closer to the scrub of trees that extended on that side. A few more shots rang out, one zipping off a stone less than a foot away.

And then it went silent.

This was almost worse than the situation he'd been in. Now they were stalking one another.

He pulled back on the bridle, the horse skidding to what seemed to be a happy stop though, immediately, the signs of agitation showed up again. He could feel the muscles of the animal twitching underneath him. She snorted, pawed at the ground. Nate hopped off her back and led her just far enough into the woods to find a decent place to keep her out of sight. He didn't think Reese would go after the horse. Maybe it was a stupid idea, but it just seemed…outside anyone's code.

Still, he lashed her loosely and then got away as quick as he could, heading deeper into the trees. The last thing he needed was catching a bullet because of a whinny.

He took a winding path, heading back toward the darker parts of the grove, all the while keeping an eye on where he guessed Reese had gone in. If he could circle around and come up behind him, things would go much differently. But if Reese had any sense at all, he would've ridden straight through and kept putting distance between himself and his pursuer.

Then again, Nate thought as he picked his way through the trees, doing his best to avoid the brambles and dead leaves, Leon

Reese hadn't shown anything but desperation in the last little bit. Maybe this was Nate's chance to put his icy resolve to its best use.

He crept up toward a small stream. The fewer trees weren't exactly what he wanted, but the gurgling of the water over the stones was. Any sound could give him away and it was a trade-off he was going to have to make. He hunkered down. It was the same choice he'd been making since the last time he'd been in Boulder Pines. Was the risk worth the reward? Today, most definitely.

He sat still for a moment, one hand splayed on the ground, the other on his revolver, listening.

Then he heard it.

It wasn't a guarantee, but it was the best bet he had. Nate crept forward, keeping low to the ground, his gun now out and at the ready.

It was a chuff. Not a sound that should've mattered any other time, in any other place. But there were only two horses out here, and Nate knew his was too far away from the sound to carry.

He hunkered down even further, covering the distance between them at almost an excruciating pace. It was the same problem as always. Take too long and Reese would bolt. Go too fast and Nate would give away his position.

He reached up slowly and moved the branches of a bush aside, a dark shape ahead of him in the trees.

And there he stood. The man who had ruined his life. The man Nate had been chasing after for years. The man who, stupidly, had his back turned to the bounty hunter and his gun barely in the holster.

His free hand clenched at his left bicep and Nate could see the glimmer of blood in the afternoon light that cascaded through the trees. He eased the hammer back on his revolver, so very aware of every click it made. Reese kept his gaze forward, wiping his hand on his pants every few seconds.

This was almost too easy. Nate lined up his shot.

And stopped.

You're going to shoot an injured man in the back? He could practically hear his father's voice ringing in his ears. *What justice is that?*

Nate paused, not lowering his gun, but easing off the trigger ever so slightly.

What would be justice here? Death in the woods? That would make Nate feel better, at least for a moment. He felt a chill run down his spine when he realized what he really wanted, and wondered what kind of person he'd become. He'd chased Leon Reese for so long, and he was hardly the only person Reese had impacted. No, if he was going to be just, if he was going to be fair, this man needed to spend every day thinking about his crimes, the same way Nate and dozens of others had done.

He stood up, bringing his revolver in front of him, but his finger resting on the trigger guard. "Leon Reese," he started.

And that's when Reese's horse made a break for it.

He should've known better. He'd assumed the animal wasn't tethered so Reese could make a quick getaway. Instead, it was serving as his last gang member, the one who would spook easiest and give him a warning if things went wrong. And they'd gone so wrong.

The horse galloped blindly, toward Nate instead of away as he would've hoped. He dove to his left, cracking his elbow and shoulder on the stones in the shallow pond and, more importantly, soaking both revolvers in the process. The shots rang out immediately, but they were sporadic, and not aimed. The thing that had saved him had been the thing that was now causing him the most problems. The creek wasn't deep, the banks were only a foot or so high, but he was now unarmed outside of his pocket knife, and that wasn't much up against a revolver.

Nate stayed still for a moment, letting Reese wonder. Then he made his move.

He was up and running in an instant, taking a few loud steps through the water before diving over the creek bed, rolling, and popping up as close to where he'd been as his disorientation would allow for. The scramble through the brush hadn't done him much good, but one look at Reese told him what had.

Wasted bullets. The man had one good arm and an empty gun. He was trying frantically to hold the barrel between his legs and reload the chambers, but he was shaky from loss of blood and nerves. The bullets slipped between his wet fingers. In an act of desperation, he threw the gun at Nate and turned, obviously hoping to make it back deeper into the woods, to any place Nate might lose him.

In a way, he almost felt bad. The man was bleeding and barely able to run a straight line. Nate was on him in an instant, tackling him from behind and driving them both to the ground. He felt the warm blood on his hands as he jerked Reese onto his back, pinning the man's arms with his knees and raising his own fist in the air. He leaned his weight on the fresh wound in Reese's arm.

"Okay, okay," Reese tried to raise his hands, but Nate's weight had him nearly immobile.

Thankfully, Nate had seen this before. He reached back, feeling inside the man's boots and, sure enough, there was the knife.

"Leon Reese," Nate held the knife up, looking at the blade. It almost glimmered in the sunlight. "I've been looking for you for quite some time now."

The man laughed. "That's your line, huh? Well, yeah, you and everybody else out here. You're lucky you didn't find me without a hole in my arm. This woulda gone a darn sight different."

"You don't know how it's going to go yet." Nate leaned forward, the tip of the knife against Reese's throat. He could see the blood pulsing there. He knew exactly where he needed to put it and it would be so simple.

Then he saw the arrogance in the man's eyes.

"Well go ahead and do it, ya coward. You've been looking for me. Let's see if you got what it takes."

Nate pressed the blade forward, slowly. And just slightly. Just enough to prick the skin, enough to get a bead of blood to trickle down Reese's throat.

"Oh, I got what it takes," Nate said. "I've been learning that ever since you killed my family. Now," he flicked the blade to the side, drawing a little more blood but barely giving the man more than a scratch, "I reckon it's time to see if you do. So far, I put in many long years. I reckon you're gonna get life." He paused. "Though maybe it'll be the rope. But I gotta be honest with you," he pulled Reese up by the shirt collar, keeping the knife less than an inch from the man's skin, "I wouldn't mind letting you wait it out for a while."

Nate twisted the man around, keeping Reese's good arm pulled up behind his back and the knife against his throat. "I think me and you need to head back into town and see what them other folks have to say. I reckon there's some sore, new wounds there."

Chapter Ten

It was a quiet ride back to Boulder Pines. Reese had been handed over to the authorities and the local sawbones had patched him up. Nate wasn't sure if he liked that or not. He wasn't sure if he liked any of it or not. Everything that he'd wanted, or at least almost everything, had been accomplished. The gang was dead, and with their leader in lock-up, it wasn't like it was going to come back around. But he still didn't feel satisfied.

Billy had promised to take care of the undertaking situation for Dan, which really only meant they'd either be riding back up, or more likely, Nate himself would ride back, rent a wagon, and be the man responsible for moving a body across the prairie.

Sam hadn't said more than a few words, Beth even fewer.

He looked over at her. "You know, I…"

"Don't," she said, not looking over. "Not yet."

He nodded and they rode on.

***

Two weeks later, Nate was standing back on his old property. With Dan's death, and the well-wishing of Sam and Beth, the little homestead had come back into his hands. He wasn't sure what to think about it really, not yet. It was right, but it wasn't exactly right. The clip-clop of hooves caught his attention and he turned from the corral to the front of the house, a smile forming on his lips.

"Beth. To what do I owe the pleasure?"

She slipped out of the saddle, still opting for Mike's jeans, he noticed.

She shrugged. "I guess I don't know. Just seemed strange to leave you over here all alone after what you did for us."

He shook his head and looked away. "Didn't do much. Not when I was the one who took Dan out there in the first place."

"Uncle Dan," she corrected him. "He loved when you called him that. Of course he'd never tell you that. Not the big tough bounty hunter. But, Nate," she reached over and touched his shoulder, and for the first time in a good long while, he didn't jump. "You're family. He didn't have to go. None of us did. But we believe in you. We…" she looked down.

Nate started to respond, though he really wasn't sure how, when he heard another horse coming up the way. Instinctively, and for no other reason he could think of, he moved Beth slightly behind him. He held up a hand and looked at the lane.

"John Nelson?"

"Yes indeedy," the man said, leaning hard on his pommel and looking like the ride had taken more out of him than the horse. "You're a hard fella to track down, y'hear?"

"I mean," Nate looked around. "I guess I can give you that. What brings you to town?"

"Well," Nelson sat up in the saddle, somehow appearing immediately more sober. "I got a bone to pick with you."

Nate moved Beth further behind him. "Is it about the steak? You said raw as dough. I didn't figure it was my place to question a man's opinions."

"Well," Nelson said again, making Nate reconsider the man's level of liquor. "Thing is," he rested his hands on his hips. "I think you may have done me a bit of a disservice."

"How's that?"

"Ya see," and that's when Nate did indeed see. He saw so many things. He saw Nelson's eyes clear. He saw the man's hand rest on the butt of his gun. And most importantly, he saw a picture in his mind of the peg inside the door, the one that was a good twenty feet away, and the one that had his gun belt hanging on it.

"I ain't exactly one for adventure," Nelson started up again. "But I am one for business. And ya did me a bit of trouble when you took out my best client."

"You were in cahoots with Reese?" It was, as they said, implausible, but not impossible.

"Why do you think he kept coming up 'round my way? I told you before. I sit at the tables. I know the secrets. I just pass along what I think might be useful."

Nate could feel Beth lean up against him, getting behind his shoulders, a hand reaching out to take his. "So why tell me?" he asked, though he felt he already knew the answer.

"So you'd get yourself good and dead," Nelson said. "You ain't been exactly helpful to me. And to be frank, this wasn't exactly a ride I was looking forward to." The man pulled the revolver from his holster and pointed it at Nate. "Fact is, I wasn't really interested in your lady friend there, but I reckon if she stands close enough I might get you both done with one bullet and we can put this to rest. But if it makes you feel any better,

I'll pop her before I take off anyway. No sense in wasting a trip."

Nate felt something cold in his hand and realized just why Beth had reached out for him. It wasn't comfort she was looking for. She wasn't asking for anything. She was giving him something.

"I suppose that's true, John," Nate said, looking over at the man. "I appreciate you helping me out."

The movement was quick, so quick Beth would later tell him she didn't quite realize he'd done it until the body toppled off the back of the horse.

Nate looked down at the small gun in his hand then turned back around, taking Beth in his arms. "This is what you've been practicing with? No wonder you're such a good shot."

"Fits in my handbag," she went up on her toes and kissed him. "And comes in useful every now and again."

"Are you looking over my shoulder right now?"

"Hasn't moved since he hit the dirt."

"You're a very unique young lady."

She pulled back. "After a rather individual young man."

***

It was another two weeks before they could get things planned. Bob needed to sign paperwork; Nate needed to get the house ready. And Beth had a dress to attend to. But finally, a month after they'd put Reese behind bars, and after what felt like a lifetime of searching for him, Nate Carson carried his bride across the threshold and felt like he was home.

He kicked the door shut behind him, looking down at her in his arms.

"You're really gonna make it as a farmer?" she asked, looking up at him. "No more adventure? No more running around the country? Just a plain old husband?"

He glanced over his shoulder to where the gun belt hung by the door. "You never know, but I'd say I'm ready to give it a try."

She pulled him down to give him a quick peck on the cheek. "Well, just so you know, the rifle's in the closet. No sense in it getting rusty."

He laughed and carried her upstairs.

Printed in Great Britain
by Amazon